Frightening Florida

ISBN 978-0-9846528-8-4

Printed in the U.S.A.

First Printing, August 2013

Table of Contents

Destinations of Doom

Frightening Florida

by
David Anthony
and
Charles David Clasman

One:
Deep Green Sea

Pensacola, FL
September 9, 3:45 pm

Emma Garland stared at the Gulf of Mexico from the backseat of her family's minivan. The Gulf's normally brilliant green waters were dreary and black.

"What's up with the water?" she asked her parents in the front of the van.

"It sure is gloomy," Mrs. Garland agreed.

Mr. Garland chuckled in the driver's seat. "Don't worry, ladies. The hurricane just stirred up the Gulf a little. It'll settle back down in a day or so."

"I hope you're right," Emma said. "It looks nasty."

This region of Florida was called the Emerald Coast. The

water along its sandy white beaches was usually bright and tinted green. The nickname had been given to the area in 1983 by a junior high school student. A contest had been held to invent a slogan for the area to attract more tourists.

"Da-da-da-da!" Emma's baby sister Dora cooed in the car seat next to her. The eleven-month-old couldn't talk yet, but that didn't stop her from trying. Or from making a lot of noise.

"That's right, honey," Mr. Garland said in his best baby voice. "Daddy will keep you safe from the hurricane monster."

Dora squealed, grinning from ear to ear.

"How much farther?" Emma asked.

"About fifteen minutes," Mrs. Garland replied patiently. She had already answered the same question half a dozen times during the five-hour drive.

"Good!" Emma said with relief. "I can't wait to get out and stretch. I think every part of me is asleep."

"Let's just hope that Hurricane Hillary didn't blow away our house," Mr. Garland joked. "She was a big bad wolf filled with hot air."

"That's not funny," Mrs. Garland frowned.

Mr. Garland turned in his seat to wink at Emma. To his wife, he said, "Alright, alright. I'm sure the house is okay. The hurricane was barely a category two. Mean old Hillary tried to take over the world, but she wasn't strong enough."

"Well, she was strong enough to force us to leave town for a couple days," Mrs. Garland corrected.

"Yes, dear, she sure was," he agreed. "Hillary chased us all the way to Grouchy Glenda's house."

"Hey!" Emma piped up. "Grandma Glenda isn't grouchy!"

Mr. Garland laughed. "That's quite a tongue twister."

"At least we were safe and sound," Mrs. Garland said.

Three days ago the Garlands had fled their home. Hurricane Hillary had been raging toward the northwestern panhandle of Florida where they lived. The family had taken refuge at Emma's grandmother's house in Crawfordville. Now that the weather had cleared, they were headed home.

"I'm just glad we had somewhere to go," Emma said. "But I'll be even gladder to get home."

"Florida can have fierce weather," Mrs. Garland said. "It has more storms than any other state." She meant especially during hurricane season, which lasted from June through November.

"That's true," Mr. Garland cut in. "But I'll take a tropical storm over a blizzard any day. I don't know how people survive in the snow. Maybe they're part polar bear."

Honnnnkkkk!

Blaring its horn, a big SUV whipped past going the other

way. Its headlights flashed crazily. The vehicle's front bumper and hood were drenched with a dripping, shiny green substance as if they had been peppered by paintball guns.

Mr. Garland slowed, swerving to avoid the careening SUV. "Whoa! What's that guy's problem?"

"Maybe he's trying to tell us something," Mrs. Garland suggested. "That's the first car we've seen in a long time. There could be trouble up ahead."

"Yeah, trouble if I catch that driver," Mr. Garland huffed. "I'll bet it was some high school punk trying to act tough in front of his friends."

"I don't know," Mrs. Garland worried. "Please be careful."

Mr. Garland grunted. "Hey, Emma, did you see the green stuff all over that SUV? It looked like a monster sneezed on it."

Emma giggled. "Yeah, Dad, it was a real booger-mobile."

"A snot-rod!" he laughed.

"A green-machine!"

"Enough!" Mrs. Garland snapped. "Really, you two, booger jokes? You're setting a bad example for the baby."

The family remained quiet for only seconds. Then Dora chirped happily. Who knew, maybe she liked booger jokes. The Garlands shared a long laugh.

Emma quieted when she gazed out the window again.

Seeing the dark water affected her mood, and her thoughts drifted gloomily.

What if the people in the SUV really had been trying to warn them about something? What if the green slime on the vehicle hadn't been paint? What if it had been something worse? Something alien? In all the stories she had heard, aliens were supposed to be green.

"Hey, Dad?" she asked softly. "Where is everyone else?"

Mr. Garland had slowed the minivan to a crawl. A trio of parked cars sat diagonally in the road. Two of the vehicles had their doors wide open. Their drivers and passengers were nowhere in sight.

"And what are those cars doing in the middle of the road?" Emma wondered nervously.

Mr. Garland exhaled slowly. "I'm not sure where everyone is. Maybe they haven't come home yet." He cautiously nosed the minivan around the abandoned vehicles. "As for these cars, well, they were probably blown around by the hurricane."

"But you said the hurricane wasn't that strong," Emma reminded him.

"Hmm, that's true," he admitted. "It wasn't. Strange."

Mrs. Garland turned and placed a hand on Emma's knee. "Don't worry, honey. I'm sure there's a perfectly good explanation for what's going on."

But Emma could tell from her mother's voice that she was worried. All of the Emerald Coast had become a ghost town. There were no other people anywhere.

Downtown Pensacola, their hometown, looked abandoned. More empty vehicles filled the streets. Businesses, homes, and government buildings remained boarded up against the hurricane. Palm trees, mailboxes, roof shingles, and garbage littered every yard and sidewalk. The city looked like the aftermath of a zombie apocalypse.

"Home sweet home," Mr. Garland announced, pulling into their driveway.

"Good thing our house didn't blow away," Mrs. Garland said with obvious relief.

"Good thing *we* didn't blow away," Emma said. "We might be the only people that didn't."

"Bah, quit worrying," Mr. Garland countered. "We'll find everyone. It'll be the greatest game of hide-n-seek ever."

Mr. and Mrs. Garland climbed out of the minivan and gratefully stretched their cramped muscles. Emma, however, barely paused. She scrambled out of her seat, dashed into the house, and flipped a switch in the entryway. Light flooded the room.

"We have power!" she cheered. Next she checked the TV in the living room. It turned on but the picture was fuzz.

None of the channels worked.

"No TV though," she sighed.

"The cable must be down," Mr. Garland said, entering the house with luggage under both arms. "That's not unusual after a storm. I'm surprised the lights work."

Emma slunk onto the couch. "This stinks," she griped. She raised her cellphone to her ear. "Maybe Layla's home."

Mrs. Garland, holding Dora on her hip, said, "The house phone doesn't work either. It's making an awful sound."

"Does it sound like crackling static?" Emma asked.

"Exactly," Mrs. Garland nodded. "How did you know?"

"My cell is making the same noise."

Smiling, Mr. Garland came inside with another load of luggage. "Mystery solved! I saw some people down the street. It looks like they're lined up outside of city hall."

"Thank goodness," Mrs. Garland said. "I didn't want to say anything, but I was a little worried."

"I set up the stroller," he said. "Do you girls want to take a walk and see what's going on?"

"That would be nice," Mrs. Garland smiled. "I could use some exercise after being in the car so long."

"Do I have to go?" Emma asked. "I don't want to leave. We just got here."

Her parents shared a quick look and they both nodded.

17

"Sure, you can stay here," Mrs. Garland said. "But don't change your mind and leave. We won't be gone long."

With no TV or phone service, Emma tried the internet. No luck there either. She was limited to playing *Angry Birds* on her cell. This might really be the zombie apocalypse!

An hour later, Mr. and Mrs. Garland hadn't returned and Emma started to worry. She stepped outside to peer down the street. Were her parents chatting with neighbors outside city hall?

Eerie silence greeted her outdoors. No birds chirped, angry or otherwise. Emma felt utterly alone. She crept to the end of the driveway and looked apprehensively left. City hall stood at the end of the block, but not a single person stood in front of it.

Was she really alone?

A furtive movement flickered in her peripheral vision. She gasped and jerked her head toward it. There was nothing there.

"H-hello?" she called.

Seemingly in response, a pitter-patter skittered across sidewalk behind her. She whipped around but saw nothing again.

"What's going on?" she demanded, becoming angry. "Who's there?"

Now she spotted it. Near a car parked half-in and half-out of the neighbor's driveway. Something green scurried out from behind the driver's side rear tire.

Emma screamed. It was a jellyfish. A jellyfish creeping across dry land on thirty wiggly tentacles. Its umbrella-shaped body was as big as a coconut and bright green like the waters along the Emerald Coast normally were.

Frozen in place, Emma screamed again. How was this happening? Jellyfish didn't walk on land! They were marine animals. They lived in the ocean.

As the impossible jellyfish approached, Emma detected a faint crackling noise. It sounded like the static she had heard on the TV and on her cell phone. The noise increased as the jellyfish scuttled nearer.

Emma didn't wait to hear more. She ran. Her parents were in city hall. They would be able to explain what was going on.

To her alarm, the jellyfish slithered after her. It moved with incredible speed and its tentacles lashed at her ankles like tiny whips. The little green brute was trying to grab her!

The garbage can seemed to appear out of nowhere. Emma tripped over it at full speed, falling with her arms out. Luckily she hit the pavement and rolled onto her back. At the same time, she grabbed the closest weapon she could find.

The lid to the garbage can.

She lifted her eyes in time to see the jellyfish launch itself into the air like a jungle cat. It was flying straight at her face! Screaming again, Emma raised the lid to shield herself and turned her head.

Splat!

The jellyfish rammed into the lid and burst like an overfilled water balloon. Emerald green slime splattered the area like a skit on a *Nickelodeon* TV show.

"Just like the SUV!" she gasped.

She realized then that the SUV she and her family had seen had been trying to warn them. Its bumper and hood had been covered in jellyfish goo.

Trying not to scream again, Emma scrambled to her feet and started to run. The now-familiar pitter-patter of jellyfish followed her. More jellies poured out of doorways, parachuted off rooftops, and scampered out from under vehicles. All of them shared a single mission.

Get the human!

Emma ran like never before. The mass of jellyfish behind her swept forward like a giant green tidal wave. The static sound crackled loudly in the air and the jellies seemed to glow electrically.

"Almost there!" Emma told herself. She was twenty feet from city hall.

In her panic, she didn't notice that the windows in the building also glowed green. City hall looked as if it belonged in the Emerald City from *The Wizard of Oz*.

Emma ducked through the glass double doors and slammed them shut. Emerald jellies smacked sickeningly into the glass. Some of them exploded in showers of slime. Others suction-cupped against the surface of the glass and flailed their tentacles angrily.

"Mom, Dad—help!" Emma cried, spinning wildly in search of her parents.

The hall was packed with people—young and old, male and female. Emma recognized many of their faces. They used to belong to her friends and neighbors.

Now they belonged to the jellyfish.

With glowing green eyes, the people in city hall wore jellyfish on their heads like bonnets. The jellyfish's slippery tentacles clung to their necks and shoulders.

"What's happening?!" Emma wailed. The scene in the hall was worse than she had ever imagined.

She whirled, intending to flee. Better to face the jellies outside than the zombie people inside.

Her family barred her escape. They wore jellyfish on their heads and their emerald eyes blazed.

Worst of all, little Dora twitched and then blinked at Emma

from her stroller. The jellyfish on the baby's head flashed with a wicked green light.

"Join us, Emma," Dora said in an awful voice like static. "It only hurts for a moment."

Emma fell to her knees, horrified. The baby that couldn't speak had spoken. If the jellyfish could do that to a baby, what would they do to her?

The End

Two:
Secret of the Sinkhole

Gainesville, FL
May 4, 2:11 pm

Brady Thomas picked a ripe orange from a low branch and cocked his arm back like a quarterback in the big game.

"Calvin, go deep," he called to his friend.

On cue, Calvin Lyons started sprinting down a row of overgrown orange trees. He waved a hand while looking back over his shoulder.

"I'm open!" he shouted.

Brady tossed the orange with practiced precision. It sailed crisply through the air, arcing toward its target. Calvin cupped his hands and prepared to make the easy catch.

"Interception!" a third boy cried.

His name was Troy Polacek and he suddenly burst from behind a tree. He had been waiting to ambush his friends. He leaped between Brady and Calvin and caught the orange in a dazzling display of athleticism.

"And the crowd goes wild!" he cheered, spiking the fruit on the ground with a *splat*.

"It's about time you showed up," Brady said to Troy.

"Me?" Troy said. "What are you talking about? I've been here for over an hour. You guys are late."

"We had a hard time getting in," Calvin admitted. "We had to sneak. The police have the whole orchard blocked off."

Brady caught up to his friends and shoved Troy playfully. "How'd you get past the cops?"

Troy grinned and shrugged. "That's my little secret. Maybe I have special powers that I can't tell you about."

Now Calvin gave him a shove. "Hey, Brady, listen to this. Troy thinks he's a ninja."

"Well, I could be," Troy said. "I could be anything. You guys would never know."

"You're special, all right," Brady laughed, rolling his eyes.

"Yeah, well, you guys didn't find what I found," Troy told them.

"What's that?" Brady challenged.

"The new sinkhole," Troy replied.

The smiles on Brady and Calvin's faces vanished instantly. The boys were done with silly. Sinkholes were serious! They usually occurred when underground water washed away the limestone below the surface. Without the limestone to support it, the ground collapsed into the space below, forming a sinkhole.

"Where is it?" Brady and Calvin demanded. "Take us to it."

Troy tilted his head and pretended to consider their request. He frowned, seemingly in deep thought.

"I don't know," he said slowly. "A ninja shouldn't reveal his secrets."

"You're confusing *ninja* with *magician*," Calvin said.

"Okay, fine," Troy gave in. "But be quiet. If anyone sees us, they'll make us leave."

"We'll try," Brady teased. "But you're the ninja. Calvin and I are just big, noisy football players."

The truth was they were all football players. Brady and Calvin had been best friends since kindergarten. They had met Troy last fall when he joined their travel team.

Brady was the quarterback and leader. Calvin, the biggest of the three, played offensive line. His job was to protect the quarterback, which meant protecting Brady, his best friend. Troy played defense.

The three boys crept quietly through the orange grove. The trees were loaded with ripe fruit and the tangy, sweet scent of citrus filled the air.

On the edge of the orchard stood a bright yellow farmhouse with a wraparound porch. Next to it a big, red barn—

"Whoa!" Brady exclaimed. "Where's the barn?"

The barn was gone. A roundish crater fifty feet wide plunged into the earth where the building had been. The crater—a sinkhole—had swallowed it whole.

"That's incredible!" Calvin marveled. "No wonder the police had the property blocked off."

"But where is everyone?" Brady wondered.

Two empty Gainesville police cars and an empty news van sat parked in the farmhouse's driveway. But there were no other people around, just the boys.

"Maybe the sinkhole swallowed them," Troy said, gulping air like a hungry sea monster rising from the ocean.

"How deep do you guys think it is?" Calvin asked as he cautiously approached the sinkhole.

"I don't know," Brady replied. "Maybe miles. I think I see an opening or a cave down there."

The sinkhole dropped straight down for about thirty feet. Then, instead of ending, it curved and disappeared into darkness.

Troy thrust his arms in front of his friends, holding them back. "Be careful! Don't go any closer. They live down there."

"They *who*?" Brady demanded.

"The Omnivorous Oranges of Orlando!"

Brady laughed. "That sounds like a cheesy monster book."

"Seriously!" Troy assured his friends. "The omnivorous oranges are giant worms that have lived beneath Florida for as long as anyone can remember."

"Give us a break," Brady sneered.

Calvin pointed at something on the edge of the sinkhole. "Why don't we find out for ourselves?" he announced. "There's a ladder right there."

A sturdy rope ladder hung from the rim of the sinkhole across from them. It descended all the way to the bottom where the hole curved and leveled off.

"I'm in!" Brady exclaimed, jogging around the sinkhole toward the ladder. Calvin followed him eagerly.

"You guys are nuts!" Troy shouted after them. "Sinkholes are deathtraps. You could disappear forever down there."

Brady shot Troy a surprised look. "I didn't know you were such a wimp. How are you ever going to play football in the pros?"

Troy put his hands on his hips. Brady had hit a nerve.

Playing football was Troy's dream. It was all of theirs.

"I don't care about the pros," he stated. "I'm going to play for the Florida Gators. You'll see." Brady and Calvin thought he meant the University of Florida, located in Gainesville, their home. That's where they wanted to play, too.

"Then stop whining like a cheerleader and come on," Brady admonished him.

Troy shook his head. "No way. Have fun without me."

"Whatever, you cheerleader," Brady huffed.

"Go play with your pom-poms!" Calvin taunted him.

Without another look at their friend, the pair scrabbled down the ladder. Brady, always the leader, went first. Thirty feet was farther than it looked and both boys were breathing heavily when they reached the bottom.

They peered dubiously into the tunnel that opened in front of them. Darkness peered back.

"Are we *sure* there's no such thing as omnivorous oranges?" Calvin asked nervously.

"What are you, Troy's twin?" Brady asked sarcastically. "I don't want you becoming a cheerleader too."

"I'm just saying," Calvin defended himself. "This tunnel doesn't look natural. It looks like something made it."

Brady pulled out his cellphone and used its flashlight app

to brighten the smooth limestone passageway.

"We're here to find out," he said, starting forward.

Calvin hesitated. "I don't know."

"Remember, there are a bunch of cops down here," Brady reminded him. "They have guns and stuff. Giant worms don't stand a chance against them."

Calvin exhaled and reluctantly followed his friend and quarterback. He wished he had a flashlight or a cool app on his phone.

The tunnel burrowed through solid limestone. Its smooth surface looked almost polished, and the boys' footfalls echoed in the darkness with each step. No other sound emanated from the black abyss.

Were Calvin and Brady really alone? What about the police? The news crew? Maybe Troy had been right about the sinkhole being a deathtrap.

A voice called from the darkness ahead.

"*Help!*"

Calvin gasped. "Did you hear that?"

Brady cocked his head, listening.

The call came again, fainter but still recognizable.

"*Help!*"

"Who do you think it is?" Calvin whispered.

Brady shrugged. "Does it matter? Someone is in trouble

and we can save them. Just think of the news headlines: *Local Football Stars Rescue Victim Trapped in Sinkhole.* We'll be heroes!"

"I guess," Calvin said unconvinced.

After a short walk, the tunnel opened into a cavern as large as a high school gymnasium. A dozen other tunnels connected to it like the spokes on a wheel.

"Is this where the omnivorous oranges meet up?" Calvin murmured.

Brady ignored him. He jogged toward something lying on the far side of the cavern. It looked like a black box with a blinking red light.

"Check it out," he said when he reached the object. "It's a TV camera."

"But where's the TV crew?" Calvin wondered, squinting fruitlessly into the various black passages.

"Let's see if we can get it to work," Brady suggested. "Come here. I'll hold the light."

The boys squatted next to the camera. Brady held his cellphone aloft while Calvin fidgeted with the camera's buttons.

"Here, I got it," Calvin said, pushing rewind and then hitting play.

An image appeared on the camera's small viewscreen. It showed a female news reporter clutching a microphone. She wore a suit and looked professionally attired, but her face was ghostly white. Her eyes widened in panic.

"They're everywhere!" she screamed into the camera. "I can't count them all! There's too many! The police are trying to hold them off, but—"

The camera's angle suddenly lurched sideways and the picture turned black. The sounds of screams and police gunfire erupted in the darkness. Then the playback stopped.

Brady and Calvin stared at one another in silence for only a moment. The camera had told them everything they needed to know. *More* than they wanted to know. Something had attacked the police and news crew. Something deadly.

"We have to get out of here!" Brady howled. "Run!"

He grabbed Calvin's arm and sprinted toward the exit. They didn't get far.

Creatures darted into the chamber from every tunnel. But they weren't giant orange worms like Troy had predicted. They were a Florida legend come true. A Floridian nightmare.

Gatormen!

Brady had heard stories about Florida's gatormen, especially about their most famous specimen, Jake the Alligator-man. He had never expected to see one up close and very personal.

The monsters were half alligator and half human. They

had shrunken human heads covered in scales and mounted on small gator bodies. Their front legs were arm-like but could propel the beasts quickly as they scampered on all fours. Their hateful eyes were as black as night.

Brady and Calvin huddled in the center of the chamber. The swarm of gatormen surrounded them.

"Please don't eat us!" Brady wailed.

"We don't taste like chicken!" Calvin howled.

The gatormen pressed in closer. Their breathing sounded like hissing. Their reptilian bodies smelled like a swamp.

To the boys' astonishment, one of the gatormen pushed itself upright and stood on its hind legs. Its baleful face met Brady and Calvin's.

"We don't eat slaves," it hissed dryly. "Unless they prove to be useless."

"S-slaves?" Brady stuttered.

"Yes, slaves," it rasped. "Kept to dig our tunnels."

Human slaves digging tunnels! Could that be how sinkholes were really formed?

Calvin, still holding the news camera, heaved it at the gatorman standing on two legs. The sudden attack caught the monster off-guard and knocked it to the limestone floor.

"Run, Brady, run!" Calvin yelled.

Head down, he plowed into two gatormen that blocked

the exit tunnel. Calvin was an offensive lineman, after all. He knew how to push people—including alligator people—down. The three of them fell in a tangle of snarls and grunts.

He also knew how to protect Brady, his quarterback.

"Go!" he cried as the gatormen slithered over him and pinned him to the ground.

Brady bolted. He ran through the hole that Calvin had opened toward the main tunnel. The light from his phone flickered wildly with the motion of his stride. Behind him the creatures roared in disapproval.

"Get it!" the lead gatorman bellowed. "Stop that human!"

But Brady was fast, a true athlete. He leaped over the gatormen blocking his way and dashed into the tunnel. Up ahead the tunnel's exit shined with the light of day. It was his goal line, his end zone, and his escape. He prayed he would make it in time.

He burst through the tunnel's opening and the brilliant daylight stung his eyes. He tripped, fell to his knees, and covered his face. But he had reached the sinkhole. The ladder to the surface couldn't be far away.

"I told you not to come down here," hissed a familiar voice.

Brady pried open his eyes.

Troy lay on his belly in the bottom of the sinkhole.

"What?" Brady muttered. "What are you doing on your—
"

His eyes adjusted to the light and his words died.

Troy wasn't lying on his belly. He was standing on all fours like an alligator.

"What are you?!" Brady wailed.

But he knew the answer. Troy was a gatorman, just like the monsters in the tunnels! Somehow he could change his shape.

Worse, Brady also knew that Troy was here to prevent him from running away. Troy was a defenseman on the football field, and at the bottom of a sinkhole.

Brady squeezed his eyes shut again helplessly. He was going nowhere until the other gatormen arrived.

The End

Three:
Monster Mansion

Orlando, FL
February 15, 5:08 pm

Jason Price and Christian Lee gazed up in awe at Orlando's newest attraction, *Monster Mansion.*

It was a menacing sight.

The tall building looked like a classic haunted house. Shadows painted the exterior black and thick draperies in the windows hid what lurked inside. Six slender chimneys were scattered across its gabled roof. They spewed silvery vapors like ghosts into the darkening sky.

"I can't wait for it to open," Christian said, breaking the silence. "It looks awesome."

Jason shook his head. "Don't hold your breath," he

muttered. "This place has been 'coming soon' for months."

"Bummer," Christian complained.

"There's no opening day listed on the website either," Jason continued. "No date, no countdown. Nothing!"

"Double bummer," Christian grumbled.

"You said it," Jason agreed. "But we have to get in there. And we have to be first. Our readers are counting on us."

The boys considered themselves theme park experts. From Disney World to Universal Studios and to everywhere in between, they'd done and ridden it all. In fact, they wrote a column in their middle school newspaper about the best and newest attractions in Orlando. The articles were very popular.

Christian stared up the wide wooden steps at the entrance to the mansion. Broad double doors with large brass door knockers stared back. The heavy doors looked like they would creak when opened.

"Have you tried knocking?" he asked.

Jason cocked his head thoughtfully. "I dare you," he challenged.

So Christian shrugged and strode up the steps. He was a big kid with all the courage that usually came with it. Not much scared him.

Until today.

He raised one thick fist, preparing to knock.

"You dare me or what?" he asked Jason.

His friend didn't have time to reply.

The double doors swung open, creaking exactly the way Christian had suspected they would. He winced but held his ground.

An elderly man's pale face peered out from the darkened doorway. The man had black hair streaked with gray and a thin mustache. He wore a somber gray suit like a funeral director. He arched one slender eyebrow inquisitively at Christian.

"Can I help you?" he asked in a low, raspy voice.

Christian stammered and turned to his friend. He was brave enough to knock on the door, but he hadn't really expected anyone to answer. He had no idea what to do or say next.

Jason did. "When does the Mansion open?" he blurted.

The elderly man's wrinkled face looked thoughtful as he studied the boy. Then he glanced at a clipboard in his hands and frowned slightly.

"I'm afraid the Mansion isn't ready for guests," he stated, flipping through the pages on the clipboard. "Some of the exhibits remain … incomplete."

"That won't bother us," Jason said quickly. "Besides, we would love to help. We're journalists. We write for the school paper."

The man looked up sharply from his clipboard. "Are you volunteering?" he inquired.

"Yes, absolutely," Jason said without hesitation.

"Sure," Christian concurred.

"Excellent," the man nodded. "I accept your offer. Please follow me." He turned and started to shuffle down the hall beyond.

The boys scrambled after him excitedly. They couldn't believe their luck. They were going to be the first visitors inside *Monster Mansion.* Of course they would help. They would do almost anything for an opportunity like that!

"This is going to be awesome!" Jason whispered to his friend.

"Thanks to me," Christian said.

"What?" Jason wondered. "Why?"

"Because it was my idea to knock."

"Like you're the first person to think of knocking on a door," Jason said.

"No, not the first," Christian seemed to agree. "But I did think of it before you."

"Well, I'm thinking of doing some knocking too," Jason admitted.

"Yeah, on what?"

"On you," he said, playfully shaking a fist at his big friend.

The dimly lit hallway led straight into the mansion. It had no other doors or turns. Framed black and white photographs of classic monsters lined the walls. Jason spotted the Wolfman, the Creature from the Black Lagoon, the Mummy, and the Invisible Man.

The elderly man stopped them in front of a cordoned waiting line that zigzagged back and forth. Thick black rope was draped between waist-high wooden poles. Carvings of leering gargoyles squatted menacingly on the tops of the poles.

"Welcome to *Monster Mansion*," the man announced, bowing slightly. "I am Victor Franklin, the proprietor of this establishment. Once you pass through this line, a car will be waiting to take you into the depths of the mansion. I usually recommend that guests remain seated at all times."

Christian nodded eagerly. "Sounds simple," he said.

"Yeah, we know how it works," Jason assured Mr. Franklin. "Sit down and buckle up. We're experts, don't forget."

"Then I suggest you begin," said Mr. Franklin.

Whooping with excitement, the boys charged through the cordoned line. They skidded to a stop at the edge of the tunnel on the far end, their tennis shoes squeaking on the hardwood floor.

The tunnel ran left and right into darkness. Rollercoaster-like tracks extended along it in both directions. The design was common and the boys had seen it many times during their amusement park adventures. What surprised them was the car on the tracks.

It was a lidless coffin.

Set on six shining chrome wheels, the coffin-car glided noiselessly to a stop in front of them. The vehicle's polished body was as black as a raven's eye. Jason and Christian's images were reflected on its mirrored surface.

"Awesome," Jason whispered in awe.

Christian nodded in agreement. "Let's do this," he said.

They flopped heavily into the front seat of the coffin-car. As amusement park authorities, they always rode in front. The back and middle seats were for chickens.

When the boys lowered the safety bar, the car started silently forward. They passed into the tunnel and were swallowed immediately in darkness. The opening was like a mouth that devoured light.

Jason shivered. "I can't see anything in here," he complained. "Is it supposed to be this dark?"

"You're not scared already, are you?" Christian teased.

"Watch it," Jason warned him.

Suddenly the coffin-car swerved sharply right and thick

strands of something unknown slapped against the boys' faces. Was it cobwebs? Seaweed? Braided human hair? Jason and Christian weren't sure they wanted to know.

The light returned, though, pale and ghostly. A waning crescent moon hung low overhead, revealing a startling scene.

They were outside.

In a graveyard.

"Whoa!" Jason gasped.

The coffin-car slowly snaked between rows of weathered tombstones. As it approached the center of the cemetery, it slowed and glided to a stop.

Christian gripped the safety bar and shook it impatiently. "Move!" he ordered the car. "The ride just started."

"Is this supposed to scare us, Mr. Franklin?" Jason called out. "Sitting in a graveyard? We're not afraid!"

Despite his confident announcement, he peered around, squinting into shadows. The cemetery seemed deserted. But Mr. Franklin had to be controlling the car from somewhere nearby, didn't he?

A rustling sound came from behind them. The boys twisted in their seats, unable find the source.

"Mr. Franklin?" Jason tried again.

Still no answer.

The rustling, though, came again. A lot of it. The scratchy

sound emanated from all around the stationary car.

"Hands!" Christian shouted.

"Feet!" Jason shouted in response. "What? Wait! What are we talking about?"

"Look at the ground!" Christian stabbed a hand over the rail of the car. "Hands are sprouting up everywhere!"

Not just any hands. They were dead hands. Boney hands. Hands covered in gray flesh like undercooked meat.

Jason screamed. He couldn't help himself. The awful hands looked so real.

More rustling filled the night air as dozens of gruesome hands broke the surface of the earth. Filthy arms started to appear as well. They stretched toward the dark sky with a purpose from beyond the grave.

Even the normally fearless Christian's face paled. "Why won't this car move?" he snarled, shaking the bar again.

And just like that, it did. The coffin-car jerked to life like the undead hands. It rolled toward a dark stone archway in the outer wall of the mansion. A barred gate in the arch rose like a garage door, providing entrance to the gloomy building.

"Here we go again," Jason grinned at his friend.

"Bring it on!" Christian hooted.

The pair was over their fright and ready for the next scare. Or so they thought.

The coffin-car whizzed them through the arch and back into the mansion. They arrived in another long hallway. More framed monster photographs were hanging on the walls, but the boys sped by too quickly to identify them.

The car was really zooming.

"Hang on!" Christian cried.

Jason grabbed his friend's arm tightly with both hands, howling in mock fright. Christian shrugged him off.

"Not to me, you goober!"

Laughing, Jason threw his arms above his head as if they were riding a rollercoaster. "Whoohoo!" he cheered.

The hallway ended at an open door. The tracks continued through it. So did the coffin and its riders. They streaked through the doorway and raced down a steep ramp on the other side. The boys' stomachs leaped into their throats.

They really were riding a rollercoaster!

The ramp twisted like a waterslide, tossing them from side to side in the speeding car. No wonder Mr. Franklin told riders to stay in their seats!

When the ramp leveled off, the car glided to a stop in a long rectangular room. Jason guessed they were deep underground. The room had cement block walls, no windows, and crackling fluorescent lights. It looked like a laboratory.

For a mad scientist.

A marble table stretched nearly all the way across the room. One half of it was covered with glass beakers, test tubes, leather-bound books, Bunsen burners, and strange devices Jason couldn't name. The other end was suspiciously empty. Four thick chains dangled unused from its sides.

The boys waited patiently, but nothing spooky or surprising happened in several minutes.

"*Boooring!*" Jason proclaimed in a singsong voice.

"Yeah, this must be one of the incomplete exhibits," Christian observed.

"Guess so," Jason agreed. Then he smiled. "But maybe we can help."

"How?"

"I'm not sure yet," Jason said. "Let's get out and take a look."

"Sounds better than sitting here," Christian said.

When they climbed out of the car, though, something finally happened.

Everything all at once.

The lights went out. The Bunsen burners flared. And a bolt of fiery blue lightning flashed between the electrodes of two metal contraptions on the table.

Hissing angrily, the bolt fractured like a crack in a car windshield. One jagged arm struck Jason. Another hit Christian.

Both boys convulsed and then went rigid.

After the lightning faded, the overhead lights swelled, coming back on. Jason gasped for breath. Smoke rose from his clothing, but he was alive. He patted his chest and thighs to be sure. He patted his shoulders, his back—

He froze. His back was *huge*. A large hump bulged between his shoulders. It had never been there before.

And now that he was thinking about it, he realized that he was standing sort of hunched over. He couldn't straighten his back no matter how he tried.

"Christian!" he yelled, starting to panic. "Something's wrong with me!"

A deep snarl came from the table, accompanied by the rattling of chains.

Christian lay chained there, only it wasn't Christian. Not anymore. The lightning had transformed him into a green monstrosity with bolts in its neck.

Gasping again, Jason fell to his knees. "This can't be happening," he muttered. "This isn't real."

"Igor, is that you?" Mr. Franklin asked, striding into the room wearing a white lab coat.

Jason's mouth moved, but nothing coherent came out. He was too stunned, too shocked, too terrified to speak.

Christian was a monster and he was … what, a hunchback?

Mr. Franklin smiled at Jason. "Igor!" he cried in greeting. "So good to see you!"

Jason shook his head, still speechless. *Igor?* Christian flailed and shook his chains.

"And there's my monster!" Mr. Franklin exclaimed, gazing fondly at Christian. "I'm so happy you boys volunteered. Now my Mansion is complete."

And with that, he raised a pencil to his clipboard and checked the final two items off his list.

Lab Assistant Igor.

Doctor Frankenstein's Monster.

The End

Four:
Old George

Sanibel, FL

April 12, 11:30 am

Eddy Cabrera had a passion for adventure. He loved combing the beach for lost treasure and island hopping on his Uncle Rico's sailboat. It didn't matter where he went so long as it offered the chance to discover something valuable.

And all his hard work had finally paid off.

"We're going to be rich," he told his friend Riley.

"How rich?" Riley asked, pedaling hard on his rusty old BMX bike. He was struggling to keep up with Eddy's newer road bike.

"Rich enough to buy you some better wheels," Eddy grinned. "And a yacht for me. Now come on and keep up."

"I'm trying!" Riley huffed, pumping harder. "But I think you're getting a better deal."

It was an incredible day for exploring. It was a perfect seventy-eight degrees with no clouds in the sky and no humidity.

The boys had been riding most of the morning. They had left home early and set out for the J. N. Darling National Wildlife Refuge, also known as the "Ding." The Ding was famous for its many kinds of migratory birds and its natural mangrove forests.

Cruising down Memorial Wildlife Drive, Eddy and Riley could understand why so many people visited the Ding every year. The lush beauty of the park was breathtaking.

"Is your uncle working today?" Riley asked. Eddy's Uncle Rico was a Ding park ranger.

"No, he's out sailing."

"But aren't you his first mate?" Riley wondered.

"He took his new girlfriend," Eddy shrugged. "They wanted some alone time."

"Oh," Riley said, rolling his eyes.

"Exactly," Eddy nodded. "Grownups!"

"So when are you going to tell me about your secret discovery?" Riley prodded his friend. "You know, the one that's going to make us rich."

Eddy pointed ahead. "The answer starts up there on that sign," he said.

The boys coasted to a stop in front of a warning sign that depicted a cartoon alligator. The gator had bottles in its stomach to represent food. Bold words read, "Caution: $500 fine. Don't approach, feed, or harass the wildlife."

"Is that your Uncle Rico's girlfriend?" Riley laughed, gesturing at the alligator on the sign.

Eddy chuckled too. "Yeah, she's a real man-eater!"

The boys snickered until they heard an enormous splash. Something big was moving toward them through the nearby water.

"Wow!" Riley exclaimed, spotting it first. "That's the biggest gator I've ever seen!"

A monstrous, seventeen-foot alligator eyed him from the shallow water. The huge reptile appeared to grin, displaying rows of massive teeth.

"Hey, I know that gator," Eddy said, climbing off his bike and approaching the water's edge. "It's Old George. Uncle Rico says he's lived here longer than anyone can remember."

"You know that monster?" Riley said doubtfully. "You're kidding! Or is it your uncle's girlfriend?"

Eddy chuckled again. "Honest," he said. "Uncle Rico called him Old George and said he was harmless."

"Harmless?" Riley shook his head. "I don't know about that. Look at those teeth. They're giant."

"The bigger the teeth, the older the gator,"

Eddy intoned.

"So Old George must be ancient," Riley marveled. "I bet he belongs in the *Guinness Book* for the most gator birthdays!"

"You mean hatchdays," Eddy corrected. "Reptiles have hatchdays instead of birthdays."

"Whatever," Riley said. "It looks like he's smiling."

"That's how he cools off," Eddy said. "By sitting with his mouth open. But he actually wants to play fetch."

"What!? Get out of here."

"I'm serious," Eddy replied. "Watch."

Eddy picked up a fallen branch from the ground and tossed it into the leafy brush. It splashed into the dark water with a noisy plop. As soon as it struck, Old George took off as if he were shot out of a cannon. He snatched the branch in his powerful jaws and—*chomp*!—swallowed it.

"Whoa!" Riley gasped.

"It's not real fetch," Eddy explained. "It's more like plop-n-chomp. Old George will gobble up anything that makes a big plop in the water."

"I hope this isn't your secret plan to make us rich," Riley said. "A circus gator named Old George? I think every gator in the world will eat whatever plops into the water."

"No, Old George isn't the secret," Eddy said, stepping into the muddy water and pushing through the mangrove branches. "He guards the secret. Come on. I'll show you."

"In there? Not a chance," Riley said. "No way am I going in there with Old George on the loose."

The alligator had returned and was lying lazily about twenty feet away. Its big, toothy grin looked fearsome, not friendly.

Plop! Another splash caught the gator's attention and it slithered off to investigate.

"We're totally safe, you big baby," Eddy teased his friend. "Old George will leave us alone as long as we toss something into the water once in a while."

Riley sighed. There was no talking his adventurous friend out of this. "I'm glad you told me to wear boots," he muttered, reluctantly following Eddy into the swampy vegetation.

As the two friends splashed along, the road and all signs of civilization quickly disappeared. The thick forest and murky water seemed to belong to another age. The boys felt like the explorers of long ago. They quickly lost track of time.

"How did you ever find anything back here?" Riley wondered.

Eddy tossed another stick that landed with a far-off plop.

57

"Uncle Rico gave me the tour. I worked with him the other day. That's when he introduced me to Old George and to Sunset Rock."

"Sunset Rock?" Riley asked. "What's that?"

"Take a look," Eddy pointed. "It's right there."

Through the dense vegetation, a large orange object became slowly visible. It was a huge, clay boulder the size of a dump truck. It stood partially submerged in the water like the setting sun disappearing behind the horizon. It rose above the surrounding mangroves like a giant.

"That's it," Eddy announced. "Sunset Rock."

"It's huge," Riley commented in astonishment. "How'd it get here? It doesn't look like it belongs."

"I know, right?" Eddy agreed. "It looks like it fell out of the sky."

"Sure does," Riley said, rubbing a hand on the rock's unusually smooth surface. "But how will it make us rich?"

"Are you sure you're ready to know?" Eddy grinned.

Riley made a fist. "Start talking," he threatened jokingly.

"I did some research after Uncle Rico took me here," Eddy explained. "And I discovered that this rock is the secret to the Fountain of Youth."

Riley gave him a questioning look. "What are you talking about? The Fountain of Youth is supposed to be in Saint

Augustine. There's even a park there. That's on the other side of the state."

Eddy threw another stick into the water to make sure Old George was busy. "Well, sure," he said. "That's where Ponce de Leon searched first."

"First?" Riley asked curiously. "Ponce de Leon discovered Florida. He could have searched anywhere he wanted."

"Exactly," Eddy smiled. "And he did. After searching the east side of the state, he sailed here to Sanibel Island."

Riley waved an impatient hand, knowing there was more to Eddy's history lesson. "You'd better talk fast before Old George comes back hungry."

"So Ponce de Leon sailed here," Eddy explained. "He and his crew tried to land twice but failed. They were attacked by the Colusa Indians both times. Ponce de Leon actually died from the wounds he received in battle."

"Get to the point," Riley said.

"Think about it," Eddy told him. "Ponce de Leon came here after searching Saint Augustine. He didn't find the Fountain there because it was *here* and he knew it."

Riley thought for a moment, absorbing Eddy's story. Finally he asked, "Even if that's true, what does it have to do with this rock?"

"I'll show you," Eddy answered, turning and starting to

navigate through the tightly packed mangroves around Sunset Rock.

"You said that already," Riley reminded him.

A clearing opened up into a small lagoon on the other side of Sunset Rock. It was cast in shadow by the colossal rock. In the center of the lagoon rose a small, lush island filled with color.

A narrow beam of sunlight shone on one small patch on the island's surface. It extended from a slender hole that burrowed through Sunset Rock. The beam illuminated a tiny gurgling spring. Water bubbled up from it like a drinking fountain into a clear pool as big as a bathtub.

"Do you see it?" Eddy exclaimed. "I was right!"

Riley nodded silently, unable to speak. Had he and Eddy just found the real Fountain of Youth?

The boys eagerly sloshed through the knee-deep water of the lagoon. White pelicans scattered out of their path. They climbed onto the flowery island and the impossible little fountain burbled before them. It was theirs for the taking.

They had discovered a legend.

"We're going to be famous!" Riley cheered.

"And live forever!" Eddy added. "But don't forget the most important part."

"What's that?" Riley asked.

Eddy slapped him on the back. "We're going to be rich!"

He knew that Florida had more retirees than tourists and alligators combined. He and Riley could make a fortune selling the Fountain's water to senior citizens. The elderly would pay dearly to be young again.

"Now be careful," Eddy advised, opening the backpack he wore slung over his shoulders. "And put this stuff on. The water from the Fountain is magical but dangerous."

"Okay," Riley nodded, barely taking his eyes from the Fountain.

They pulled on plastic rain ponchos, goggles, and rubber gloves over their clothing. Eddy had stowed the gear in his backpack.

"What else is in there?" Riley asked.

"Empty water bottles," Eddy answered. "A dozen of them. We'll fill them and take them back." He took a brief look around. "Okay, there's no sign of Old George. Let's do this."

Riley nodded and pulled up the hood of his poncho. Carefully he and Eddy filled all twelve plastic bottles with the precious water from the Fountain of Youth. They concentrated and finished quickly.

Capping the last bottle, Eddy let out a long sigh. "Success!" he breathed.

"You mean 'money, money, money!'" Riley sang, helping

Eddy fill the backpack with liquid gold.

Splash!

Suddenly a broken tree limb crashed into the pool on the island. The Fountain's water surged into the air, drenching the boys from head to toe. Their protective gear didn't repel it all. The mystical water soaked their exposed skin.

"*Nooooo!*" Eddy wailed.

"What now?" Riley shrieked. "What do we do?"

Eddy's eyes searched desperately for a solution. With a sinking feeling, he spotted a familiar toothy grin.

Old George.

The huge alligator lay in a sunny spot on the shore of the lagoon. His grin looked as proud as a pat on the back.

Eddy understood instantly.

"It was Old George!" he cried. "He knocked the branch into the pool on purpose."

"So what do we do?" Riley repeated.

"Get in the lagoon! Wash! Try to wash the water off!"

Eddy and Riley scrambled off the tiny island and into the dark water of the lagoon. They scrubbed and scrubbed but the Fountain was working its magic already. No drinking required.

"I feel funny!" Riley howled, and Eddy felt the same. His clothes felt baggy and loose. His backpack grew heavier and heavier. It slid off his shoulders with a thump.

Eddy was shrinking!

"You look like a kindergartner!" Riley screeched.

"So do you!" Eddy sobbed.

The boys were growing younger. Years reversed with each passing second. Soon they were toddlers.

All because of Old George.

"Oh, man!" Eddy shrieked. "I never expected this to—!"

His words trailed off into a series of noisy squeals and goo-goo's. He couldn't talk anymore. He and Riley were babies.

With noisy splashes the babies teetered and fell into the water. They were too young to stand.

Plop! Plop!

One cue, Old George slithered into the lagoon. He glided along the water's surface toward the babies. It was time for another game of plop-n-chomp.

The End

Five:
The Pirate and the Prism

Key West, FL
April 2, 11:02 am

"Hurry up already," Mia McVeigh urged her cousin Jack. "Unroll the map. I want to see where it goes."

Kneeling next to her, Jack struggled to unroll the ancient parchment. Its stiff, yellow paper crinkled noisily and felt glued together. "Hold your horses," he said. "I don't want to tear it. The map's really old, you know."

Mia sighed anxiously and toyed with the rusty skeleton key that dangled from her necklace. "We have just over two hours. My mom and dad told us to be back at 1:30 for lunch. I want to find the treasure before we run out of time."

Jack finally unrolled the map.

"You worry about the key," he told her, squinting at the strange symbols and writing on the paper. "I'll worry about the map."

"Well then?" she asked. "What's it say?"

He glanced up at Fort View Trail ahead of them and pointed. "It says to go that way."

The cousins started marching side by side down the sandy trail. The way meandered through a wild tangle of tropical vegetation. Rich green shrubs and vines crowded evergreens and palm trees. Multicolored birds sang cheerfully all around, safe among the leafy shelter.

"This place is magical," Mia marveled at their surroundings. "I bet it's filled with lost pirate treasure."

"You're probably right," Jack agreed. "Fort Taylor used to be an outpost in the battle against pirates."

"Yeah, I know," Mia said shortly. "I heard what the tour guide said, the same as you. Just imagine how many pirates used to roam this area back then."

Fort Taylor, where the cousins were visiting, was named after President Zachary Taylor. It had been built because of its important naval location on the island of Key West. The area was a natural gateway between the Gulf of Mexico and the Atlantic Ocean. It had also been a route frequently used by pirates.

"This way to the treasure, matey!" Jack directed, turning sharply onto a narrow path that branched off the main trail. "Keep up, lass, me booty lies ahead!"

"Don't you mean *our* booty?" Mia said. "I have the key, remember. If you forget, I'll kick you in the booty."

"Aye, matey, our split will be fifty-fifty," he agreed in pirate-speak. "Me booty don't need a kickin'."

Mia laughed. "Nice pirate imitation, but don't quit your day job. You won't be winning any contests soon."

In response, Jack closed one eye tightly and let out a big "*Arrr!*"

Mia shook her head and laughed again.

It was fun to be away from home, she thought. She was having the best vacation ever, especially now that she and Jack were on a real pirate adventure.

Mia and her parents lived in Jacksonville, Florida. Every spring break they traveled south to the Florida Keys. It was a family tradition. It was also a tradition to bring Mia's cousin Jack along. The kids were very much alike and they both loved pirates.

This year they had stopped at a flea market in Key Largo on their way down. A strange man dressed in a colorful costume had sold Mia and Jack an old treasure map and skeleton key. He had known little about the items. He told the kids that a parrot had dropped them on his head at the beach.

On examining the map, the kids discovered an X over Key West where they were going. Maybe it was luck, destiny, or a little of both. Only time would tell.

Mia followed Jack from path to path on a journey that seemed longer than possible. The wooded area around Fort Taylor wasn't vast. How could their trek be so long?

"This is it!" Jack shouted excitedly. The trail they were currently following opened up to a sandy shoreline. "This is where the trail ends. On this beach. X marks the spot."

"Okay, but *where* on this beach?" Mia wondered, looking up and down the long stretch of sand. "It's miles long."

Jack studied the map. "I'm not sure," he admitted. "There's just a big X right—"

Squawk!

A large blue parrot squawked noisily overhead and the cousins stared at it curiously.

"This way to the treasure," the bird chirped. "Follow me, follow me!"

Mia glanced at her cousin. "Do you think that could be—" she began.

"—the same parrot?" Jack finished.

They meant the same parrot that the man at the flea market had encountered. The one that had dropped the map and skeleton key. Finding a talkative parrot in the middle of nowhere seemed like too much of a coincidence.

"Hey, look, it's changing color," Mia said.

As they watched, the parrot's feathers morphed from robin's egg blue to fire engine red.

"Aww," Jack complained. "I hope the parrot isn't supposed to be the treasure. Not even if it does change colors. I want gold."

"I think it's cool," Mia said.

The parrot squawked again and then flew off north along the shore. A short distance down the beach, it circled and looked at the cousins.

"This way!" it beckoned. "Follow me, follow me!"

"Do you think it knows where the treasure is?" Mia asked.

"If it does, then I'm a scurvy dog," Jack snorted.

Mia smirked. "Get ready to bark," she said. "I mean, look, it talks and changes color! It has to know something."

She was right about one thing, at least. The parrot had turned yet another color. Now it was banana yellow.

"Fine," Jack huffed. "Let's see where it goes."

"Awesome!" Mia cheered.

They followed the bird along the coastline for about fifteen minutes. All the while, it squawked and talked, promising treasure just ahead.

Eventually the now-cucumber-green parrot landed among the fronds of two solitary palm trees. The trees' trunks crossed, forming a giant, natural X.

"X marks the spot!" Mia exclaimed. "I told you the parrot was cool!"

Jack grinned at Mia and then at the bird. "It isn't just cool. It's awesome!"

Squawk!

The parrot, now as white as vanilla ice cream, liked their thinking.

"Dig here!" it cawed. "Dig here! Treasure!"

"That parrot's awesome, but it's pushy too," Jack noted.

"Oh, well," Mia shrugged. "Help me dig."

The cousins dropped to their knees between the crossed palm trees and started to dig. They used their bare hands. The sand was loose and dry, making the work easy.

They sang a song from one of their favorite pirate books as they knelt in the sand:

Sail with me through the Sandy Sea.
For a fee you can sail with me.
Swab the deck.
Mop up every speck.
Double check or you'll sleep on deck.

The hole was over two feet deep when Mia's knuckles rapped against something solid.

"I think this is it," she said eagerly. "It looks like you really are a scurvy dog, Jack. But I knew that already."

"If we find treasure, you can call me whatever you want," Jack answered.

Working faster now, they cleared away the sand and uncovered a trap door. The solid wood bore a faded painting of the Jolly Roger on its surface. The skull-and-crossbones seemed to leer mockingly at them.

"Treasure!" the golden parrot squawked. "Open it, open it!"

Jack glanced over his shoulder. "Okay, okay!" Jack snapped. "We're working on it."

"Open it, open it! Treasure!" The bird was becoming hysterical.

"Can you shut that thing up?" Jack muttered.

"What's wrong?" Mia teased. "Is the parrot making you cuckoo?"

Jack groaned.

"Forget the bird," Mia said, changing the subject. "How do we open the door? There's no handle."

Jack peered into the sandy hole, examining the door closely. After a moment's study, he smiled.

"Try the key," he said. "There's a small hole in the skull's eye patch. I bet it's for the key."

Mia had forgotten about the skeleton key around her neck. She pulled it off the string while Jack moved aside.

"Here goes," she said, leaning in.

She gently inserted the key into the hole in the eye patch and turned her wrist. *Click!* The door sprang open immediately, moaning like an angry spirit. A gust of stale air blasted Mia and Jack in the face. They fell back on their pockets in the sand.

"Whew!" Jack gasped. "What a stink!"

"It smells like the door hasn't been opened in years," Mia gagged, covering her nose.

"Weird," Jack said.

Mia nodded. "All of this is weird, especially that crazy parrot. Look at it now. It's as pink as a flamingo."

"Never mind the bird," Jack said. "Let's get the gold."

"And the diamonds," Mia added.

"And the rubies."

"And the—"

"What about the pirate?" said a voice from the space below the trapdoor.

The cousins scurried to the edge of the hole and peered inside. Perhaps seven feet below them stood a man. He had a long, scraggly beard and wore a pirate's costume. A tri-cornered captain's hat sat askew on his head. The space below was otherwise empty.

"Ahoy, me hearties," the pirate greeted them. "I be the one and only Captain Filch. Pleased to make yer acquaintance." He bowed dramatically, tipping his hat.

Mia and Jack fell silent, both at a loss for words. They'd never expected to find a living pirate beneath the sand!

"How's about helpin' me out?" the pirate said. "I been down here a long time."

Mia nodded and brushed her sandy hands off on her thighs. "Sure, of course. Let me give you a—"

Jack, though, swatted her hands. "Are you crazy, Mia?" he roared. "We don't know him or how he got down there."

"Oh, that's easy to explain, lad," Captain Filch said smoothly. "I was trapped here by a witch doctor. He used voodoo on me and stole Prism, me beloved bird."

"Is Prism a parrot that changes color?" Mia blurted.

"Aye, that be her," the pirate nodded. "Have ye seen 'er?"

"How did you survive without food or water?" Jack demanded.

"I told ye, boy," Captain Filch explained. "The witch doctor used voodoo."

Jack shook his head doubtfully. "I … I'm not sure I believe

you," he murmured.

"What's to believe?" the captain chortled. "I'm stuck in a hole and I need yer help. How's about it?" He raised a hand hopefully.

Finally Mia shoved her cousin aside. "Ignore him," she apologized. "And forgive us. We should have helped as soon as we saw you."

She knelt at the edge of the hole again and extended a hand to the pirate.

"There's a good lass," Captain Filch said, gripping her hand. "Now pull if ye don' mind."

Mia did as asked, but she wasn't strong enough to drag the grown man out of the hole by herself.

"A little help?" Captain Filch asked Jack.

"Fine," the boy said reluctantly. He offered a hand to the pirate who clutched it with his free one.

"On three," the captain grinned. "One, two …"

Before he reached *three*, Prism the parrot landed on the hat on his head. The mysterious bird was now as black as a raven.

"There's me purdy lady!" the captain exclaimed. "It's about time too."

Flash!

A sudden burst of blinding white light pulsed around the

parrot. Mia and Jack squeezed their eyes shut against it. When they reopened them, everything had changed.

The pair was huddled in the empty space below the trapdoor. Captain Filch leered at them from above like the Jolly Roger skull. Prism sat perched on his shoulder, back to her original blue color.

"What?" Mia gasped.

"How?" Jack wondered.

They had traded places with Captain Filch. They were stuck in the hole and he was free!

"Thanks for the rescue," the pirate said, seeming very far away. "And thanks to Prism fer makin' it all possible. She can change more than 'er color, ye see." He stroked the parrot's blue head with one finger.

While the cousins tried to figure out what that meant, Captain Filch kicked the trapdoor shut with a booted foot. Darkness filled the small space below and the sound of shoveled sand rained down on the trapdoor.

The End

Six:
Mother's Day

Daytona Beach, FL
May 11, 4:45 pm

"Jackpot!" Alexander Hernandez exclaimed, dropping to his knees in the sand.

"Wow!" his sister Isabelle marveled. "I've never seen so many in one place before."

The pair knelt on the sandy white beach with an open backpack between them. Sand dollar shells were strewn throughout the sand around them like chips baked into cookies. The kids couldn't believe their luck.

"It's like they know tomorrow is Mother's Day," Isabelle said.

"Who, the sand dollars?" Alex asked, making a face.

"That's goofy. Sand dollars aren't alive and they don't have moms."

"They used to be," Isabelle corrected. "Alive, that is. They were sea urchins. That means they had moms too."

Alex stared at her as if she were crazy. "Whatever," he finally said.

Sand dollars—flat, coin-shaped shells found on ocean beaches around the world—wash onto shore and are bleached white by the sun. The Hernandez kids were collecting them for a Mother's Day present for their mom.

"'Whatever' yourself," Isabelle retorted. "Mom's going to be so surprised. We'll be able to use these to decorate a lot of stuff in her shop."

"Yeah," Alex agreed with a grin. "And you know what that means."

"That Mom will be happy?" Isabelle guessed.

Alex snorted. "Sure, that too. But it'll mean cash for us. Mom always pays for the shells we bring her."

"Come on, Alex," his sister scolded. "Stop thinking about you. This is for Mom. Tomorrow is *her* day."

"I know, I know," Alex said, raising his hands defensively. I was kidding … sort of."

"Sure you were," she said.

"I was," Alex shrugged. "But there's nothing wrong with

making Mom happy and earning a few dollars at the same time. It's a win-win for everyone."

"Dollars for dollars," Isabelle grinned.

"That's right," Alex said. "Dollar bills for sand dollars. Sounds like a good trade to me."

The kids' mother, Mrs. Hernandez, owned a tourist shop that sold T-shirts, alligator-shaped hats, '*I ♥ Florida*' coffee mugs, and tiny sailboats in glass bottles. The shop also sold items decorated with sand dollars, including picture frames, vases, water pitchers, and jewelry boxes. Such items were always popular.

"I think we have enough," Alex said as he scooped up a final handful of the shells. "Any more and I won't be able to carry the backpack. Let's go home."

"We still have to buy flowers, don't forget," Isabelle reminded him.

"I didn't forget," Alex protested. "Don't be so bossy."

"I wouldn't be bossy if you weren't forgetful," she fired back.

"Bossy Beth."

"Forgetful Frank."

Alex slung the bulging backpack over his shoulders and gazed around in mock confusion. "Looks like I forgot the way home. Why don't you lead, Sister Sassy?"

"Fine by me, Brother Bonehead," she smiled.

After they crossed the beach, they walked along the sidewalk toward South Atlantic Avenue. *Floral and Hardy's*, the flower shop, was only a block away. Nevertheless, it took them over an hour to agree on what to buy.

They finally decided that Isabelle would pick the flowers and Alex would choose a card. She arranged a cheery bouquet of purple and pink orchids. He selected a sand dollar-shaped Mother's Day card. It seemed fitting.

They arrived home about an hour before their mom.

"Hide the flowers in your room," Alex said, clutching the backpack by a strap in front of him. "And I'll find somewhere to put these."

"Now who's being bossy?" his sister teased.

"Just do it," Alex said.

"Can't," Isabelle replied. "We have to wrap them."

Alex nudged the backpack with a knee. "What's wrong with giving them to her like this?"

"You're kidding, right?" she laughed. "They're presents. Don't be such a boy."

"Whatever," he shrugged.

The sand dollars fit neatly into four shoeboxes. The wrapping was also neat, at least after Isabelle took over.

"The tape goes on the boxes, not your fingers," she told

Alex. "Haven't you ever wrapped a present before?"

"I'm more of a receiver than a giver," he explained slyly.

"Nice attitude," she said. "Keep it up and you won't be receiving any presents ever again."

The pair finished just minutes before Mrs. Hernandez came home. They tucked the boxes under Alex's bed and put the flowers and card in Isabelle's closet. Everything was ready for the morning.

Dinner and the evening passed unremarkably. The kids watched TV until bedtime, eager for the morning to arrive.

Shortly after 1:00 am, though, Alex awoke with a start. Strange noises filled his dark bedroom. He lay in bed, frozen with fear, imagining aliens trying to abduct him.

A dry scratching sound drifted out from beneath the bed. Hearing it caused Alex to think of fingernails clawing against a closed coffin lid. It was the sound of trying to escape after being buried alive.

"W-who's there?" he croaked, his throat tight and barely able to force out the words.

The tear of paper was the only reply. Whatever had been trying to escape had succeeded.

Alex held his breath, waiting for what would happen next. Five seconds passed. Ten. He broke out in a cold sweat beneath the sheets.

Suddenly the clacking of tiny feet skittered across the hardwood floor of his room. It sounded like dozens of feet at first, then hundreds or maybe thousands.

When the sound faded, he forced open his eyes, dreading what he would see. What had invaded his room? Could it be aliens? Wiggly insects on nasty little legs? His sleepwalking sister?

Something lay on the floor next to his bed, a black shadow in the dark. It was oddly-shaped but didn't move. No wiggling there.

He squinted at it and let out a breath.

The shoeboxes full of shells! They had been dragged out from under his bed. And, by the look of them, their wrapping paper had been shredded.

"How did that happen?" he murmured.

Someone had gotten into the gifts, but who?

As if in answer, a shadow appeared in his doorway. It filled the space momentarily and then slid silently into his room like a ghost.

Alex was about to shout when—*click!*—the light came on.

"What's going on?" his sister asked from just inside the doorway. Then she noticed the torn presents on the floor. "Oh, no! Alex, what did you do?"

"It wasn't me, I swear," he said, sitting up. "I think something in those boxes was alive."

His sister shot him a skeptical look. "What are you talking about?" she demanded. "We wrapped the boxes ourselves. There was nothing in them but shells."

"I know, but—"

Alex snapped his mouth shut when a loud hissing came from down the hallway. It sounded like a seashell held up to an ear—but louder, much louder.

Isabelle whipped around. "What's that?" she gasped.

"It's coming from the living room," Alex whispered.

Moving closely together, they crept down the hallway. The airy hiss increased as they neared the living room.

"Hit the lights," Alex said softly.

Isabelle did as asked, the room lit up, and Alex was sorry immediately.

A swarm of ghostly-white creatures scurried across the floor, the walls, and the ceiling of the living room.

Sand dollars!

Horrible mutant sand dollars!

The shells were alive and had legs—thin, spindly legs like stick bugs. They also had bulbous eyes perched on the tips of bobbing antennae along with sharp, bird-like beaks. When they opened their mouths, the hiss of the ocean poured out. When they moved, their feet made the clacking noise Alex had heard in his room.

"Yuck!" Isabelle grimaced. "Nasty! Where did they come from?"

"The beach!" Alex snapped. "It was your idea to bring them home!"

"My idea?!" Isabelle blinked.

"Yeah, you said they celebrated Mother's Day."

"I did not!" she objected. "I said—oh, forget it!"

Sand dollars started dropping from the ceiling like spiders. Some landed on her head and crawled through her long black hair. Others plopped heavily onto her back.

"Alex, help!" she shrieked. "They're all over me!"

But the sand dollars were on him too. They scurried across his head and shoulders. They scuttled up his legs.

"They're everywhere!" Alex cried, trying to fight his way to his sister's side.

He swatted at the vile things with his hands. He stomped them with his feet. But more and more kept coming, like ants swarming over a discarded crust of bread.

"There's too many!" he shouted.

Mutant sand dollars were in his shirt now. They skittered across his face. He reached for Isabelle's hand and misjudged the space between them. His shin banged against the coffee table and he fell.

Into a sea of creatures.

Alex landed on his back but didn't hit the floor. There were too many sand dollars in the way. Hundreds of the little brutes swarmed beneath him and kept him in the air like a crowd surfer at a rock concert. He lay helplessly on top of them.

"Mom—!" he started to yell, but sand dollars rapidly gagged his mouth. They pinned his lips together with their legs and prevented him from speaking.

Still struggling, he jerked his head left and spotted Isabelle in the same predicament. She lay on a wave of creatures. Her mouth was pinched shut but her eyes were wide in terror.

"*Help!*" the look she gave him begged.

He was sure his own look mirrored hers.

Like marching soldiers, the sand dollars surged forward. They streamed into the foyer, bearing Alex and Isabelle with them. Several of the critters climbed the front door and worked the handle. The rest pushed until the door opened. Then they all poured outside.

Isabelle whimpered behind her squeezed lips. Alex tried to roll over, to sit up, but he was as helpless as a turtle on its back. He grasped briefly at the door frame as he was being pulled through it. A sand dollar bit his hand with its sharp beak and he quickly let go.

The streets outside were empty. Except for the roar of the surf, Daytona Beach lay silent and asleep.

The sand dollars quickly hauled Alex and Isabelle toward the beach. The hiss from their beaks and the clack of their legs drowned their captives' muffled cries. No one would hear them scream.

When they reached the ocean's edge, the sand dollars stopped. Alex and Isabelle raised their heads to peer out into the dark water at a horrifying sight.

A huge shape rose from the depths, as big as a Volkswagen Beetle. It broke the surface like a submarine and its massive round white body glowed eerily in the moonlight. Antennae as long as cornstalks waved over it. Its glistening beak drooled.

"I-Isabelle?" Alex stammered. "What is th-that thing?"

"I think it's the mother of all sand dollars," she whispered.

It seemed the sand dollars knew it was Mother's Day after all.

And they had brought her a gift.

The End

Seven:
The Sarasota Slime

Sarasota, FL
August 14, 8:32 am

Beep! Beep! Beep!

The Batman alarm clock shrieked and Logan Pierce sat straight up in bed like the Frankenstein monster come to life. No lightning required.

"I'm awake!" he gasped, slapping clumsily at the snooze button with one hand.

He missed and the clock kept shrieking.

Beep! Beep! Beep!

So he leaned over the bed, snatched the alarm clock's power cord, and yanked it out of the wall.

Beep! Bee—!

Ahh, silence.

Logan flopped onto his back and blinked groggily at the ceiling. He was exhausted. His eyelids felt thick and scratchy. He couldn't believe it was morning already. He felt as if he had just fallen asleep.

Finally he sighed, willing himself to wake up. He was determined to get out of bed without delay. Today was a special day.

A brand new comic book store was opening in town at ten o'clock this morning. To commemorate the event, everything in the store would be on sale at half price—every comic, every poster, every trading card, and every action figure. Logan and his best friend Jared planned on being the first ones in line when the doors opened. Jared had spent the night at Logan's in preparation.

Logan yawned, stretched, and slowly sat up. He punched his *X-Men* pillow a few times, molding it into the right shape. It was time to wake his friend.

Up came Logan's arm and there went his pillow with superhero waking power.

Whump!

Smack onto Jared's unsuspecting face.

The other boy was sleeping in the twin bed across the room. And by the look of it, he was dreaming about food.

Nothing else could explain that much drool!

"Wake up!" Logan called. "You're gonna drown."

Jared rolled over and covered his head with Logan's pillow.

"Five more minutes," he mumbled.

"Not a chance," Logan replied. "We've got big plans. The early bird catches the worm, remember?"

Jared grunted. "I don't like worms," he growled. "You can have 'em. They're all yours."

That was when Logan's second pillow struck.

Whump!

But this time Logan didn't throw it or let go. He stood over Jared's bed, having a one-sided pillow fight.

"Get up," he said. *Whump!* "Or I'll unleash my titanium blades, Wolverine-style. I'm owning you as it is already." Wolverine, the clawed member of the *X-Men*, was one of Logan's favorite superheroes.

Jared snarled and leaped out of bed, driving his shoulder into Logan's chest. Playing tackle football came in handy off the field too.

Jared was a big kid, bigger than most in school. Some people even called him "The Hulk." He was *that* big. He also wore an *Incredible Hulk* t-shirt more days than not. The massive green monster was his favorite comic book character.

Logan was about the exact opposite. He was short, thin, and as hyper as a startled squirrel. He often claimed to have superhero speed.

When Jared charged, Logan flew backward and landed on his bed on his back. His superhero speed wasn't fast enough.

"*Oof!*" he grunted.

"Now who's still in bed?" Jared teased. He was smiling, so Logan knew he was just having fun.

Which made him consider raising his pillow for a friendly counter-attack. But what was the point now? His friend was awake and on his feet. Mission accomplished. The Hulk lived!

"Let's grab something to eat and get outta here," Logan grinned. "If we don't hurry, those weird old guys will get in line first. You know how hungry they are for superheroes."

To make his point, he clicked his teeth together like a chatty ventriloquist doll. *Clack! Clack! Clack!* "Nom, nom, nom," he droned with every snap of his jaw.

"Whatever," Jared said. "Just keep your teeth away from me. If you try to bite me, you'll taste a hulky hero sandwich." He held up a meaty fist to prove it.

They both laughed at that, feeling totally at ease and totally safe. Neither of them had any idea how their day would end. Nor did they know just how scary it would become.

After a quick breakfast of waffles, Logan's mom's

specialty, they hopped onto their bicycles and pedaled downtown. The morning sun shone bright and warm in the clear sky. It was the perfect beginning to the perfect day, until—

"Oh, man!" Logan exclaimed in dismay. "Look at that line! It's huge!"

"But it's barely nine-thirty," Jared complained. "The store doesn't open for thirty minutes. Why are so many people here already?"

"One word," Logan said and then the boys chanted in unison.

"*Grown-ups.*"

"They always try to buy up the good stuff," Logan continued.

"Yeah, and then they sell it on eBay," Jared scowled. "Don't they have jobs? It's the middle of the week."

Still grumbling, the boys coasted their bikes to a stop and chained them to a streetlight. They grumpily took their place at the back of the line. At least twenty waited ahead of them. *Buuuum-mer.*

"So, what's our plan when we get inside?" Jared asked. He was too excited to let the line get him down for long.

"Let's hit the back issues first," Logan answered quickly. He knew what he wanted. "You know—*Wolverine, X-Men,* the good stuff."

"Don't forget *The Hulk*," Jared said.

"He's your thing," Logan replied. "Personally, I don't get it. The Hulk is just a big dumb monster. What's so great about him?"

"What? You're crazy!" Jared retorted. "Wolverine's the dumb one!"

"You don't know what you're talking about," Logan disagreed. "Wolverine is awesome. He can heal and has killer claws. He could shred The Hulk into ribbons."

"No way! The Hulk is too strong. He would snap Wolverine in half like a twig."

Logan rolled his eyes. "Super strength, wow," he said sarcastically. "That's so original. Besides, Wolverine's real name is Logan, like me. How cool is that?"

The friends argued back and forth about their favorite superheroes for the next half hour. They argued about who would beat who in a fight. About who had the strongest powers. And about who had the coolest costume. They argued anything, really, just to pass the time.

Other customers in line tried to interject and give their opinions, but the boys ignored them. No one knew comics like they did, certainly not adults.

Finally, the time arrived. A scruffy twenty-something young man with a handful of keys unlocked the door.

"Good morning, everyone!" he greeted the people in line. "Thanks for waiting and welcome to Creature Cave Comics!" He stood aside and allowed the customers to enter.

The crowd cheered and filed eagerly into the store. Colorful posters plastered every inch of the walls. Dozens of tables loaded with long rectangular comic boxes filled the room. The boxes were stuffed with new and old issues of every comic imaginable, all of them in mint condition. The store was a collector's dream.

For the next several hours, the boys searched for those special comics that only a keen eye could find. The store didn't disappoint. It offered issues they'd never seen before and issues with rare variant covers. It was as if their birthdays had been combined with Christmas morning. What a fantastic day!

Only after they had browsed every box, table, shelf, and display did the boys finally approach the cashier.

"We're kids," Logan announced. "We're not gonna try to resell anything. Do we get a discount?"

"Sure, half off, just like everyone else," the cashier smiled.

Logan shrugged and grinned in return. "Oh, well. It was worth a try." Then the cashier rang him up and he paid.

Jared was about to pay for his purchases too, but froze. He spotted a dark green box with red radioactive symbols on it behind the counter. It was wide enough to hold comics and about a foot long. The green color made him think of the Hulk. The box had to be the only one in the store that he and Logan hadn't searched.

He pointed at the box. "What's in there?" he asked the cashier.

The cashier shrugged. "Nothing good," he sneered. "Just some independent monster comic called *The Sarasota Slime*. I think it's drawn by a local artist."

"Sarasota?!" the boys repeated with great interest. It wasn't every day that they got to read a comic about their hometown. "Can we see it?" Logan nearly begged.

"Sure, but be careful," the cashier said, picking up the olive green box and placing it on the counter. "I don't know if I'm supposed to sell these. I couldn't find them listed in the price guide earlier."

The box was metal and had a lid that opened like a trap door. Rusty hinges secured the lid to one end and an equally rusty round loop served as its handle. Intrigued, Logan pulled the lid open. The hinges screeched in protest, and he and Jared peered inside.

The comics in the box were wrapped in individual plastic sleeves. Muddy prints stained the plastic as if someone with dirty hands had recently rifled through the box—someone or *something*, Logan observed. The comics themselves were clean and dry.

Logan's eyes widened with excitement and his imagination took over. The muddy prints, he imagined, belonged to the real Sarasota Slime monster.

"These look way cooler than *The Hulk*," he said, nudging Jared in the ribs. Then to the cashier he asked, "Will you take five bucks for the whole box?"

The cashier scrunched up his face. "Come on, kid. The empty box is worth more than that."

"Ten?"

Jared slapped a twenty-dollar bill on the counter. "How about twenty?"

Now the cashier narrowed his eyes thoughtfully. "Make it thirty bucks and you got a deal. Your twenty and his ten."

"Sold!" Logan exclaimed.

The boys rode back to Logan's house with their new comics as fast as they could. There were no cars in the driveway when they arrived. A note on the dining room table read, "Went grocery shopping. Be good. Love, Mom."

"The house is ours," Logan announced. He and Jared were alone with the Sarasota Slime.

More than they realized.

Sitting on the floor of Logan's room, they dug excitedly into the green box. The rest of their purchases lay forgotten.

"The dirt on the plastic sleeves is nasty," Logan grimaced, wiping moist hands on his shirt. "Feel it. It's damp."

"I know," Jared winced. "But look at this." He wiped clean the underside of the box's lid with his sleeve. "There's a message written here. '*Private collection. Not for sale.*'"

He and Logan shared a startled look. Had they purchased something they shouldn't have?

Finally Logan shrugged. "Finders-keepers," he said. "Besides, whoever used to own these comics didn't take care of them. They're a mess."

"It's just the sleeves and box," Jared corrected, taking a comic out of its plastic. "See? The book is in perfect shape. And it looks pretty cool."

Logan leaned in, peering at the comic. The cover depicted a colorful, full-page illustration of the Sarasota Slime. The monster was a hulking man-shaped mass of green ooze that stood seven feet tall. It was shown wrestling an alligator with its massive, gooey bare hands.

"It does look kind of cool," Logan agreed. "Open it up."

The boys read eagerly, turning pages quickly. The Sarasota Slime, they discovered, had been created by a chemical spill in the Everglades. The genes of mutated frogs had fused with seaweed and mud, evolving into the monster. Now the Slime protected Sarasota from all invaders.

The boys read with nonstop excitement, soaking up every word, detail, and drawing. When they finished, Logan let out a long breath.

"That was awesome!" he admitted. "I loved it when the Slime battled those boa constrictors."

"Oh, yeah!" Jared agreed. "The Slime is so cool. It's not good or bad. It just protects its turf and takes what belongs to it."

"I really want to know what happens next," Logan said. "I hope the series doesn't—"

A sudden loud, wet sound cut him off. Both boys whirled. What they saw froze them with fear.

A slimy green behemoth lurked outside the window. The beast raised one glistening, muscular arm and smacked the glass with a sticky hand the size of a catcher's mitt. The look in its pale, fish-like eyes was utterly inhuman.

"It's the Sarasota Slime!" Logan cried. Moving without thinking, he dove toward the window and grabbed the cord to the blinds. In a panic he yanked it shut.

"What's that going to do?" Jared yelped. "We need help! Call the police—or the Air Force!"

"Where's the phone?" Logan shouted. "Find the phone!"

The front door opened and something large and heavy shuffled into the house.

"*Listen!*" Logan hissed.

The door to his room was closed, but he and Jared heard the Slime shambling toward them. The floor groaned under the monster's weight. A table creaked, shoved roughly aside.

"Oh, man, oh, man," Logan moaned.

"We're trapped!" Jared wailed.

Crawling across the floor as if to escape a fire, the boys fled into the closet. They huddled against the far wall, shivering as the door to Logan's room creaked open. The Sarasota Slime filled the doorway.

"H-help," Logan whimpered. His dry throat barely made a sound.

The Slime lumbered into the room. Its wide, wet feet slapped heavily on the floor, leaving behind a trail of gruesome slime. Its noisy breathing gurgled and reeked of swamp.

Jared clutched his friend's arm, fingers digging into the muscle. "We're not gonna make it," he croaked.

The Sarasota Slime scooped up the olive box of comics from the floor with one hand. Its other hand stretched toward the closet in a fist.

"Here it comes," Logan whispered, cringing.

The giant green fist slowly opened.

"I'm sorry for all the bad things I've ever done," Jared said.

The fist opened completely, dropping a twenty-dollar bill and two fives. Then the monster's sloppy, gooey mouth opened.

"*R-r-r-reeeeefund,*" it gurgled wetly before shambling out of the house.

The End

Eight:
Bermuda and the Beast

Miami, FL

September 7, 1:39 pm

What an awesome ride. The thirty-five-foot sailboat cut easily through the ocean swells, sending up sparkling sheets of spray. The boat's sails stretched to their fullest in the crisp wind.

And the Marshall kids loved every second of it.

"Faster, Dad! Go faster!" Ricky shouted, his eyes ablaze with excitement.

"Yeah, Dad, come on," Ricky's sister Alexis cheered. "Let's see what this baby can do!"

Mr. Marshall stood at the captain's helm and grinned fiercely at his children. His kids sat behind him on the cushioned seats in the stern, tightly clutching the rail.

"Alright, you two," he said. "Hold on!"

Then he suddenly cranked the wheel sharply to starboard.

The sailboat banked right at a 45-degree angle, slicing through the water. Alexis and Ricky's stomachs dropped and they squealed loudly. What fun! Sailing sideways was like riding a rollercoaster. The shining seawater was so close they could touch it.

When the boat straightened, Mr. Marshall flashed a broad smile at his children.

"So what do you think?" he asked, his hands never leaving the wheel.

"Awesome!" Alexis exclaimed.

"Yeah!" Ricky agreed. "This boat is the best thing you ever bought!" His shook his shaggy wet hair like a dog after a swim.

"Hey, watch it!" Alexis cried, shoving him. "I think a dogfish hopped onboard."

"*Woof, woof!*" Ricky barked, and then he puckered his lips like a fish at his sister.

Alexis shoved him again and rolled her eyes behind her sunglasses.

"I'm glad you both like it," Mr. Marshall admitted. "Because I see a lot of sailing in our future."

Ricky squinted into the distance. The ocean was an endless blue plane that met the sky at the far-off horizon. The sun sparkled on its rolling waves. There was no land in sight.

"We're out a long way," he observed, shading his eyes with a hand.

"Just a few miles," Mr. Marshall said. "Miami is back that way, to the west." He jabbed a thumb over his shoulder, pointing toward their wake. "The island of Bermuda is to the northeast and Puerto Rico lies southeast."

"Is that your way of telling us that we aren't lost?" Ricky teased.

"Something like that," Mr. Marshall agreed. "But now it's time for the question of the day. If you connect those three points, what do you get?"

Ricky and his sister stared at each other, both hoping to guess the correct answer first.

"A triangle?" Ricky blurted.

Mr. Marshall held up a hand and tilted it back and forth. "Sort of," he said. "But I'm looking for more."

"The Bermuda Triangle!" Alexis shouted in triumph.

Ricky slapped his forehead. *Curses! Foiled again!*

"Alexis wins," Mr. Marshall said. "Partial credit to Ricky."

"So what do I get?" Alexis asked. "There should be a prize for beating Ricky."

Her brother, though, changed the subject.

"Dad, isn't the Bermuda Triangle supposed to be haunted?" he asked.

Mr. Marshall laughed.

"I'm serious!" Ricky protested. "I've read that a lot of ships and aircraft go missing here all the time. We could be next!"

"You can read?" Alexis asked in pretend surprise. "Incredible!"

"Okay, you two, that's enough," Mr. Marshall interjected. "People pass through the Bermuda Triangle all the time without incident. We have nothing to worry about."

"But what about the millions that disappear every year?" Alexis asked, hoping to excite her brother again.

"*Millions?*" Ricky gasped.

"I'm kidding!" Alexis laughed. Then she blanked her face and lowered her voice. "Or am I?"

Mr. Marshall was about to interject again but a sudden strange breeze washed over the boat. He snapped his mouth shut and gripped the wheel tighter, trying to stay calm.

Ricky felt it too. The air crackled with energy and made the hairs on his arms stand up straight. He shivered but was neither hot nor cold.

"Wow, what was that?" Alexis asked, wiggling with

discomfort.

"You felt it too?" Ricky said. "Like someone walking over your grave?"

Alexis nodded. The possibility of the Bermuda Triangle being haunted seemed very real right then.

"It was a downburst," Mr. Marshall said. That wasn't accurate, but he didn't want his children to worry. "It's a very unpredictable wind. Just to be safe, I think I'll lower the sails and fire up the motor."

With an experienced sailor's skill, he quickly strode across the deck, lashing ropes and muttering orders to himself. As he tied the mainsail to the boom, the boat slowed and started to drift. Then he went below deck.

"Do you think Dad knows what he's talking about?" Alexis whispered to her brother.

"I guess," Ricky said. "I just hope that we get out of the Bermuda Triangle soon."

"You don't really think it's haunted, do you?" she asked.

"Who knows?" he shrugged. "What else could make the wind blow like that?"

"Nature," Alexis said, and then she smirked. "Or baked beans."

Ricky started to laugh, but then he spotted something dark in the water next to their boat. It floated just beneath the surface.

"Look!" he pointed over the rail.

He and his sister leaned over the edge of the boat. The object in the water was a flag. A black flag with a skull and crossbones painted on it. As they stared, it sank slowly into the depths and disappeared.

"Was that … was that what I think it was?" Alexis finally whispered.

"The flag from an old pirate ship," Ricky nodded. "A Jolly Roger."

"Awesome!" she exclaimed. "I wish we could—"

Suddenly Ricky grabbed her around the waist and dragged her to the deck like a football player making a tackle.

"Don't let them see us!" he hissed.

A dark wooden ship had appeared to starboard. The sculpture of a dragon's upper torso rose from the bow, its bat wings spread fiercely. Bearded men clutching swords and axes swarmed the deck.

"Are those Vikings?" Alexis asked in disbelief.

Before Ricky could reply, a metallic gleam caught his eye. Something was falling out of the sky. An airplane! It was painted red, white, and blue and had a propeller and dual wings. Ricky recognized it as a biplane from the early 1900s. Thick black smoke billowed behind it.

"Don't let that see us either!" he shouted.

"It's going to crash!" Alexis yelled.

"Get down!"

The Marshall kids threw themselves flat onto the deck.

"This can't be happening," Alexis muttered. "Vikings, antique planes—none of it makes sense."

"Sure it does," Ricky said. "This is the Bermuda Triangle. I told you it was haunted!"

"Fine, whatever," his sister huffed. "You were right. Do you want a cookie?"

Instead of a giant splash, though, the Marshalls heard deep voices talking. Fortunately the voices didn't sound like angry Vikings.

The kids peered cautiously over the rail. The biplane and Viking warship were gone. Instead a tan wooden canoe was gliding past their boat. It was paddled by two men who wore animal hides and had long black hair. For some reason, they paid no attention to the sailboat.

Ricky shook his head, amazed. "Those look like Native Americans," he said.

"Yeah, from the frontier days," Alexis agreed.

"But what's that behind them?"

A shadow appeared in the water behind the canoe. It was oddly shaped and rose steadily toward the surface.

"I hope it's not a sea monster," Alexis worried. After all the weird stuff they had seen, she thought anything was possible.

"It might be a shark," Ricky guessed, "or an octopus."

They were both wrong. It was a submersible—a small two-person submarine. It popped to the surface like a cork, raining water down its windowed sides. The man and woman inside wore wetsuits and pointed frantically at the sailboat.

Alexis ducked and dragged Ricky down with her. The pair huddled on deck with their backs pressed against the seats.

"Do you think they saw us?" Ricky asked.

She snorted. "Yes! What are we going to do?"

"Land, ho!"

That voice belonged to their father.

Mr. Marshall had returned to the deck. He stood at the helm, pointing off into the distance on the port side. When his kids didn't respond, he turned to them.

"Come over here, you two," he beckoned.

Ricky and Alexis shared a look and then stood up, brushing themselves off. A glance at their surroundings revealed that they were alone again. The canoe and submersible had vanished.

Ricky shivered. It seemed the stories were true. Things really did just disappear in the Bermuda Triangle.

The question was, where did they go?

"We'll be home soon," Mr. Marshall said. "There's the shore now."

A thin ribbon of coastline stretched along the horizon. Mr. Marshall had started the boat's engine and was puttering toward it.

Alexis crossed the deck and put her arms around her father. She leaned her head on his shoulder.

"I don't want to go sailing again," she said. "Not for a long time."

"Me either," Ricky seconded.

"We'll see about that," Mr. Marshall responded. "You can't let a little wind scare you."

He obviously hadn't seen what his children had. While below deck he had missed the weird sights.

They steadily approached the sandy beach. To their dismay, no docks or buildings lined the shore. No signs of civilization appeared anywhere. The beach and surrounding water looked uninhabited.

"D-Dad, where are we?" Alexis wondered nervously.

The shoreline didn't look like Miami. It didn't look like anywhere in Florida. A vast green jungle rose up beyond the beach like something from long ago.

Suddenly there came a great bellow, part elephant and

part locomotive. The trees on the beach's edge shook, scattering leaves and sticks. The greenery parted and tree limbs snapped as easily as twigs. A living nightmare thrust into view.

A tyrannosaurus Rex.

The dinosaur cocked its head, one black eye staring at the Marshalls and their sailboat. Then it reared back its head, parted its toothy jaws, and bellowed again.

Horrified, Ricky backed up even though he had nowhere to go. Nowhere he *could* go.

But he did have an answer to his question. It explained why he and his sister had seen so many strange sights that day.

Where did everything go that disappeared in the Bermuda Triangle?

To the past.

The Bermuda Triangle wasn't haunted.

It was a time machine that went one way.

The End

Nine:
Something's Fishy About Fishing

Okeechobee, FL

December 19, 7:06 am

"Dawn is the best time of day to fish," Grandpa Wormsworth said. "The second best is dusk."

"Yeah, why's that?" his grandson Denny asked.

The pair was sitting at the kitchen table on a sunny but cool morning. Grandpa was slowly sipping coffee while Denny, whose full name was Dennis Rodney Ball, munched a third piece of peanut butter toast.

Instead of answering his grandson's question directly, Grandpa asked one of his own. "Do you like your breakfast, Denny?"

"Sure do," Denny said with a mouthful of food.

"So do the fish," Grandpa said, grinning.

Denny slowly stopped chewing and smiled. "I see what you did there," he said. "The fish like to eat breakfast in the morning, same as I do, right?"

Grandpa nodded.

"And I bet they get hungry again at dusk," Denny said.

Grandpa nodded again. "You catch on quick," he said. "And I'm a morning man. The Navy taught me that. So that's why we're going to fish now."

"Sounds good, Grandpa" Denny agreed. "It's like that old saying. 'The early bird catches the worm.'"

"Uh, don't say that," his grandfather winced. "I never liked that saying. Let's use 'the early worm catches the fish' instead. What do you think?"

Denny shrugged. "Okay, sure."

His grandfather sat in a wheelchair with an American flag blanket draped over his legs and feet. The blanket was always there. Denny had never seen him without it.

What had happened to his grandfather? Denny wondered. Had he been injured during his time in the Navy? Maybe in a battle? Grandpa never talked about it. And his mother cringed and never let him ask.

"Did you do much fishing when you were in the Navy?" he asked, hoping to learn something new.

"You bet I did," Grandpa said. "Every chance I got."

"What about combat?" Denny probed. "Did you see any?"

"No, not me," he said. "I was the head cook. That's why no one cooks fish like Grandpa Wormsworth."

"You *are* the best," Denny agreed. "I don't even like fish sticks, but I'll eat everything you fry."

"Well, I don't just *fry* fish, you know," Grandpa explained. "I bake it, I grill it, I poach it—you name it. I can cook every kind of fish in every kind of way."

Denny smiled again. With Grandpa, every conversation could end up being about fish. The mystery of his legs would remain for now.

"Are you finished?" Grandpa asked, swallowing his last bit of coffee.

"Yeah. If I eat any more peanut butter, my lips will get stuck together," Denny joked.

Grandpa made a shooing motion with his hands. "So get out of my way," he said playfully. "Give me room to clean up and then we can go."

Denny stood up from the table and wandered into the living room. He knew better than to offer to help. Grandpa liked things done a certain way. If the old man wanted assistance, he would ask for it.

Grandpa Wormsworth's living room was also called the

Trophy Room. Dozens of stuffed fish mounted on plaques decorated the walls and shelves.

"What kind of fish is this?" Denny asked, staring at one of Grandpa's trophies. The fish had a striped body, a flat head, and vicious teeth. It was a fierce-looking creature nearly four feet long.

"That old devil is a muskie," Grandpa replied, cruising into the room from the kitchen on his motorized chair. "I caught him in Lake St. Clair in Michigan back in '83."

"A muskie, huh?" Denny said. "It looks more like a monster than a fish."

"It's both," Grandpa agreed. "Muskies ambush their prey. Those markings on its side are like underwater camouflage."

Grandpa certainly knew his fish. Denny was glad to learn from the best.

"Do you know what that beauty is there?" Grandpa asked, pointing at the biggest fish on the wall. It had a cobalt blue back and a silver belly. A sharp dorsal fin stretched along its spine, and a long spear-shaped upper jaw jutted straight out from its head.

"That's easy," Denny said with confidence. "That's a marlin."

"A *blue* marlin," Grandpa corrected. "They're the biggest type of marlin."

"It's huge," Denny marveled.

"Twelve feet, six inches," Grandpa bragged. "I caught that bad boy on a trip to the Bahamas."

"It must've been hard to reel in," Denny said, impressed.

"Nearly tore me apart," Grandpa recalled. "Wow, what a fight. My Navy buddies put me up to it. They bet me that I couldn't wrestle one in."

"But you showed them, Grandpa!" Denny cheered. "Because you're the best."

"Aw, shucks, boy," Grandpa said bashfully. "It's in our blood. I might be the best right now, but you'll get there soon."

"I hope so," Denny admitted.

"You will," his grandfather promised. "Trust me. You have the gift. You get it from your mother and me. It runs in the family. The Wormsworth boys are all natural fishermen, no exceptions."

The boy smiled, appreciating his grandfather's assurance. Denny didn't see Grandpa often. He lived three hours away. So it was extra special to spend this long weekend with him.

Before Denny realized it, Grandpa started wheeling for the back door.

"Let's go, boy," he beckoned over his shoulder. "The fish won't catch themselves."

Denny followed him onto the back porch and down the

adjoining ramp. The rising sun glowed orange and red across the horizon. A slow-moving canal behind the house led out to the biggest lake in Florida, Lake Okeechobee.

"What are we hoping to catch today?" Denny asked as they approached a small dock that extended out over the canal.

"Fish, of course," Grandpa joked.

"I know that," Denny smirked. "But what kind of fish?"

"The hungry kind," Grandpa laughed, slapping a hand repeatedly on an armrest of his chair.

"Real funny, Grandpa," Denny groaned.

"Hah! I'm kidding you, son," Grandpa said. "Today we'll be fishing for largemouth bass. Lake Okeechobee is full of them."

When they reached the end of the empty dock, Denny looked around in confusion. Some things were missing, he thought.

"Grandpa, where are the fishing poles and bait?" he asked.

The old man waved a dismissive hand. "We don't need any of that stuff," he said. "It's for amateurs."

"What do you mean?" Denny wondered. How were they going to catch fish without the right gear? "Are you making another joke?"

Grandpa leaned toward the boy and lowered his voice. "Are you ready to learn the family secret?"

Denny blinked. "We have a family secret? You aren't going to turn into a werewolf, are you?"

Grandpa barked a laughed. "Heavens, no! You read too many monster books. Not that I blame you, of course. Who doesn't like to read a good scare?"

Before Denny could reply, Grandpa adjusted the position of his wheelchair so that he was facing the boy head-on.

"So are you ready?" he asked again. His eyes sparkled with excitement.

"Um, I guess," Denny said hesitantly. His eyes, on the other hand, were full of doubt.

Grandpa patted the Stars and Stripes blanket that covered his legs. "These are the family secret, Denny. They're pretty special."

"Your legs?" Denny asked, puzzled. "I don't understand. I thought your legs didn't work."

"Oh, they work just fine," Grandpa said. "Here, take a look!"

With a quick gesture, he pulled the American flag blanket away from his body. Beneath it lay a horrible surprise.

Worms.

Grandpa's legs and feet were slimy giant earthworms!

Denny lurched violently backward and tripped onto his rear.

"Grandpa, your legs!" he exclaimed. "Something's wrong! We have to get you to a hospital!"

Grandpa chuckled and his wormy legs stretched toward Denny like curious elephant trunks.

"Well, would you look at that?" he beamed. "They're happy to meet you."

"Gross, no!" Denny cried, swatting at the worms—his grandfather's legs—whatever they were.

"Oh, quit being a baby," Grandpa scolded him. "You're a Wormsworth, the same as I am. You'll get your new legs when you turn sixteen."

"My new legs?" Denny whined. "Do you mean that's going to happen to me too?"

Grandpa smiled and patted his squirmy legs the way he would pat a family pet.

"You'll be an amazing fisherman, Denny," he grinned. "I told you it runs in the family."

The End

Ten:
The Witching Hour

Tampa, FL
January 13, 8:04 pm

Someone was stealing Dominic Renaldo's Legos. First a few of his medieval knights had disappeared. Then pieces from his Star Wars set. The thief had struck five times on five consecutive nights.

"It's Shannon," Dominic told his father after dinner. "I just know it. Who else could it be?"

Mr. Renaldo tried not to grin. His son blamed almost everything on his six-year-old sister Shannon.

"Do you have any proof?" Mr. Renaldo asked in a neutral tone.

Dominic sputtered, turning his hands palms up. "No, but

who else could it be?" the boy repeated.

"Maybe you loaned the Legos to a friend and forgot," Mr. Renaldo suggested. "Maybe to Joey? Or to Mark?"

"Nope," Dominic said, shaking his head vigorously. "I never loan them to anyone. I don't want the sets to be incomplete."

That was probably true, Mr. Renaldo silently agreed. His son was a Lego fanatic. The only place the kid ever wanted to go on vacation was to Legoland in Winter Haven, Florida.

"Have you checked the ocean?" Mr. Renaldo said, a grin finally curling his lips. "Your Legos could have been sucked into—" He lowered his voice to a spooky whisper. "—*the Bermuda Triangle*."

Dominic shot his father a sour look. "Be serious, Dad."

The Bermuda Triangle was a supposedly haunted region in the Atlantic Ocean to the east of Florida. Many ships and aircraft were said to have disappeared there.

Mr. Renaldo shrugged, still grinning. "What can I say, Dom? Your Legos will turn up. All of your misplaced toys do."

Dominic wanted to argue, but he knew he wouldn't convince his father. His Legos weren't misplaced. He was very careful with them. Someone was stealing them and he was determined to find out who.

He stood up from the table. "I'm going to bed," he said.

His father looked surprised. "But it isn't even eight o'clock and it's the weekend."

"There's nothing else to do," Dominic said. That wasn't his real reason for going to bed so early, but it was easier than explaining.

Once Dominic was in his room, he shut the door, locked it, and turned off the light. He slipped into bed still wearing his clothes and set his alarm clock for 11:59 pm. The Lego thief had struck after midnight for five straight nights. Tonight Dominic would be waiting.

When the clock buzzed, Dominic opened his eyes immediately. He felt as if no time had passed and that he hadn't slept at all. His nerves were tightly wound. He lay in a ball and clutched a flashlight with fresh batteries against his chest under the blankets.

"Okay, thief," he whispered in the dark. "I'm ready. Come and get it."

There was no response.

Long minutes passed and Dominic fought the urge to sleep. Lying alone in the dark wasn't exactly exciting. The only light in his room came from the soft blue display of his clock. The minutes ticked by slowly.

At 12:21 am, he realized it was the Witching Hour. That

was what his father called the hour between midnight and 1:00 am.

"The Witching Hour is when the night is most dangerous," Mr. Renaldo had told his son on many occasions. "Especially for kids. It's when bad things happen to those who aren't sleep."

Dominic knew the Witching Hour was just a story, but he liked hearing about it anyway. His father enjoyed playing tricks on him and trying to scare him. Dominic liked it too.

Hoping to entertain himself, he stared at the dimly lit ceiling and let his mind wander. He thought about his father, the Witching Hour, and his missing Legos. Then an idea struck him.

His father was stealing his Legos! That's why he hadn't helped Dominic find the thief. He *was* the thief. He was responsible. It was another one of his pranks.

Dominic smiled to himself, pleased that he had figured it out. His next move would be to invent an appropriate counter-prank. He had to think of a fun, sneaky way to get even with his father.

A sudden high-pitched creak broke the silence. Dominic recognized it but hadn't expected it. The door to his closet was opening.

He froze, eyes wide and breath caught in his chest.

Someone was in his room! Someone who had been hiding in his closet.

The intruder moved slowly, trying to be quiet. Nevertheless, the floor groaned softly. Dominic's heart started to race. The intruder was getting closer. The heavy scent of wet dog filled his nostrils.

Unfortunately, Dominic and his family didn't own a dog.

The intruder stopped on the far side of Dominic's bed. Its heavy breathing filled the air like the hissing of a giant snake. Dominic didn't look yet, but he heard the intruder grunt as it reached for something on the floor.

His Legos. He stored them in a plastic tub under his bed.

With a *snick* the lid to the tub popped open and then the clack and rustle of Lego bricks confirmed Dominic's suspicions. The intruder was the Lego thief!

Dominic sat up sharply and flicked on his flashlight. He expected to catch his father in the act. Who else would play such a trick on him?

Instead he saw a nightmare.

There was a monster kneeling beside his bed! A monster with green skin and pointy tusks jutting out of its mouth. It had its long, gangly arms buried in Dominic's Legos. For some reason, it was wearing blue pajamas covered in baseballs like polka dots.

When the monster saw Dominic awake, it screamed. Dominic screamed, too, and dropped his flashlight. The light went out immediately, plunging the bedroom into darkness.

"Dad!" Dominic hollered, yanking the blankets up over his head. "Mom! There's a monster in my room! From the closet!"

A noisy clash of sounds echoed through the dark. The clatter of spilled Legos. The thump of the monster as it scuttled across the floor. Dominic's terrified screams. The bang of his father pounding on the door.

"Open up!" Mr. Renaldo shouted. "Unlock this door!"

Now that his father was there, Dominic found his courage. In one motion, he threw off the covers and leaped out of bed. He scampered across the room, flipped on the light switch, and whipped open the door.

He pointed at the closet. "It's in there!"

Mr. Renaldo made a puzzled face. "What is?" he demanded.

"The Lego thief," Dominic explained rapidly. "It's a monster."

His father frowned. "You had a nightmare," he said. "There's no such thing as monsters."

"You're wrong," Dominic disagreed. "I didn't have a nightmare. I *lived* one! Just look at my Legos. Look in my closet!"

Knowing his son wouldn't go back to bed until he checked the closet, Mr. Renaldo strode across the room. He pulled the door wide and peered inside.

What a mess. The closet was as disorganized as a laundry hamper. A heap of clothes, papers, books, and discarded toys hid the floor completely. Very few clean shirts hung on hangers. Even fewer toys sat on the shelves.

About the only thing Mr. Renaldo didn't see in the messy closet was a monster.

"You're cleaning this tomorrow," he said. "First thing. And lay off the scary stories for a while."

Dominic sighed loudly but didn't protest. He wouldn't win this argument either.

"Go back to bed," Mr. Renaldo continued. "We'll keep your door cracked and leave the hall light on." He clicked the light switch in Dominic's room off. "Now try to get some sleep."

Dominic flopped heavily into bed and rolled onto his side. The display on his clock read 12:39 am. It was still the Witching Hour.

After several minutes passed, Dominic slipped out of the covers and scooped up his flashlight from the floor. He knew what he had seen. A monster in his closet. He wasn't going to let it steal his Legos anymore.

He drew open the closet door and shined his light up, down, left, and right. He saw no sign of the intruder.

"It's sneaky. I'll give it that," he said out loud. Then he knelt down and inhaled deeply. With the flashlight in one hand, he shoved aside the toys and things on the closet floor. The monster had to be hiding somewhere in the mess.

The small opening in the back wall surprised him. It was rough and roundish like the mouth of a cave. Dominic thought he could fit inside it if he got onto his hands and knees.

Which he did. Nothing would stop him now. The opening had to be the way the monster had crept in and out of his room unseen.

Swallowing heavily, Dominic wriggled inside.

The opening led to a tunnel that glowed with a faint white light. Jagged blue bolts like lightning flashed in the walls and ceiling, but made no sound. The texture of the tunnel was slightly squishy. It all reminded Dominic of the inside of a giant brain.

"Maybe this really does lead to the Bermuda Triangle," he whispered.

The tunnel ended at another irregular opening in another cluttered closet. But this closet wasn't made of wood and plaster. It was carved out of solid rock. A tanned animal hide hung across the doorway like a curtain.

Dominic hesitated before reaching for the curtain. His heart thumped heavily in his chest. His mouth felt hot and dry. What would he discover on the other side?

He bravely tugged the curtain aside and a dimly lit cave opened before him. Stone furnishings occupied the space—a blocky chair and desk, a bed draped with thick animal furs.

In the bed lay the monster. The beam from Dominic's flashlight shined on its ugly green face.

Dominic screamed again and so did the monster. The beast sat up, clutching the furs on its bed up to its neck. Was it afraid of him?

"Where are my Legos?" Dominic demanded angrily.

The monster bellowed again, whipping its head to the right. Dominic followed its gaze to a second doorway covered by a curtain. A louder, deeper bellow blared behind it.

Dominic froze with sudden understanding. In this strange place, *he* was the monster in the closet. He was the intruder. To the beast in the bed, Dominic's pale skin and dull teeth must have been frightening.

He also realized that the monster was yelling for its parents, just as he had yelled for his parents earlier that night.

Dominic turned and fled, losing his grip on his flashlight again. He had to get back to his room. He had to escape. The monster's father was coming.

He plowed through the first curtain and into the closet. His shins banged against the clutter as he dropped to the floor.

In the dark, the closet felt as cramped as a shoebox. Where was the opening? He couldn't find it. His hands beat painfully against solid rock.

"Where is it?" he shrieked. "Where did it go?"

To his dismay, the opening was gone. It had closed and Dominic knew why.

The Witching Hour had ended. The clock had struck 1:00 am, severing the link between his room and the monster's. The tunnel that connected them was only open between midnight and 1:00 am.

Dominic was trapped.

The monster's father roared behind him.

The End

Eleven:
The Surprised Guest

Fiona Chapel was born to sing. She had been singing for almost as long as she could speak. Now she was the lead of her middle school choir and the winner of numerous state competitions.

She wasn't just a good singer. Fiona was great.

"Will many people be at your great grandmother's party?" she asked Adriana, a fellow choir member, as the pair walked along the street lit sidewalk after dark.

"Lots," Adriana replied. "Just about everyone who lives in her retirement community will be there. Granny is really popular. She's kind of a leader."

"Maybe I should have practiced more," Fiona said nervously. "This the first time I've been paid to sing. It's different than a competition."

"Don't worry," Adriana said. "Granny will think you're the best present ever."

"I hope you're right," Fiona admitted. "It's not every day that someone turns eighty-three. I'm going to sing my heart out."

Fiona meant it. She had practiced every day for a week. In addition to the traditional *Happy Birthday*, she planned to sing a few classics like *What a Wonderful World* by Louis Armstrong.

"I'm just glad you decided to come," Adriana told her. "I wanted to bring Granny something extra special. And you're it!"

Fiona blushed and softly mumbled a thank you. She appreciated the compliment, and being paid twenty dollars was flattering.

After the girls walked two more blocks, Adriana stopped in front of an open iron gate. A gothic-looking arch above the gate bore the words *Bramsford Retirement Community*.

"Here we are," Adriana announced.

A neat cluster of homes stood beyond the gate. No streetlights lined the sidewalks. Few lights shone in windows.

Fiona thought the dark little neighborhood looked abandoned.

"Are you sure anyone lives here?" she wondered.

Adriana laughed. "We're right on time," she said. "That's Granny's house there."

She pointed at the first house on the left. It was a small, tidy home that had a short driveway filled with strange old cars. The vintage vehicles had wood-rimmed tires and hand cranks to start their engines. They reminded Fiona of buggies from the Old West.

"Wow, those cars could be in a museum," Fiona observed.

"I know, right?" Adriana agreed. "I think they're called Model T's. That's what Granny and her friends drive. They're very old-fashioned people. They don't even use electricity."

"No wonder it's so dark," Fiona said as they neared the front porch.

Adriana nodded. "They use candles and oil lamps for light. Nothing else. Granny says it creates a soothing atmosphere."

A tall man with dark, slicked-back hair opened the door before the girls knocked. He wore a black suit and matching tie. His exact age was impossible to guess. In the dim light, he could have been a college student or a senior citizen. Fiona just couldn't tell.

"Good evening, Adriana," he said slowly in a thick accent. Was he European? Russian? Fiona couldn't decide.

"I'm delighted to see you," he continued. "Who did you bring tonight?"

"Hi, Mr. Stoker," Adriana said. "This is Fiona. She's my present for Granny."

Mr. Stoker arched one thin eyebrow. "Fiona the singer? What a treat!"

"Nice to meet you, Mr. Stoker," Fiona said politely. She shook his smooth hand, which was as cold as ice.

"And it's a pleasure to meet you, young lady," Mr. Stoker smiled. "Adriana has told us all about you."

"Thank you," Fiona blushed. "I hope I live up to the hype."

"I'm sure you will satisfy," Mr. Stoker replied. "Now, please, come inside."

The girls followed Mr. Stoker into the house. Fiona was stuck immediately by how simple yet elegant it was. The furniture was made of solid wood. The rugs on the hardwood floor were hand-woven, and the heavy drapes along the windows had no embellishments.

Like the cars out front, everything in the home seemed to have been crafted in another age.

"Is Granny awake?" Adriana asked.

"Soon," Mr. Stoker answered. "You know how she loves to nap throughout the day,"

The tall man escorted them into a formal dining room.

On the long table sat a ruby red cake with stark white frosting. A mass of dark red candles was packed tightly on top. Fiona guessed eighty-three candles, the same as Adriana's Granny's age.

Also in the room sat the other residents of the Bramsford Retirement Community. There were twelve of them, all adult men and women. Like Mr. Stoker, they looked young and old at the same time.

"Oh, Adriana, she's lovely," said a thin woman with pearls around her throat.

"What a perfect gift," agreed the woman to her right.

"This will be a party to remember," stated a plump gentleman wearing a tuxedo.

Fiona flushed but returned their smiles. None of these people had heard her sing but she was already a star. She couldn't help feeling good about that. Maybe this would be her first step on the path to fame and fortune.

"Well, I am pretty good," Fiona admitted.

"And so young," Mr. Stoker said. "Just how old are you, dear, if you don't mind me asking?"

"Thirteen," Fiona answered. "But don't worry. I've been singing since I was a baby."

"Thirteen is excellent," Mr. Stoker assured her. Then he reached toward the cake and started plucking candles from the top. The other people seated around the table counted out loud as he did so.

"One," they chanted in unison.

"Two." Their voices grew louder.

"Three." The woman with the pearls started to rock excitedly in her tall chair.

When they reached thirteen, everyone applauded. Their eyes blazed and sweat stood out on many of their timeless faces.

Fiona glanced at Adriana. "What was that all about?" she whispered.

"It's a family tradition," Adriana explained. "Granny doesn't like to think about getting older on her birthday. So we take candles off her cake instead of adding more."

"But why thirteen?" Adriana asked.

"Because you're the guest of honor and you're thirteen," Mr. Stoker interjected. "You will make all the difference tonight."

Suddenly the plump man in the tuxedo hissed. "*Shhh! She's coming.*"

"It's time," Mr. Stoker announced. He quickly lit the candles on the red-and-white cake with long wooden matches.

As he finished, a beautiful woman glided into the room. She moved so smoothly that she seemed to be floating. Her pale skin was like porcelain, but her straight black hair was as dark as a raven. She wore a long, lacey black gown that trailed behind her like a wedding dress.

"Happy birthday!" the guests cheered.

The woman nodded slowly then raised a hand for silence. The room quieted instantly. She glanced at Fiona and then at Adriana.

"What do we have here?" she asked.

"Your gift, Granny," Adriana said. "Happy birthday!"

Fiona shot Adriana a shocked look. This beautiful woman was her great grandmother? This was *Granny?* She looked younger than Fiona's mother. How could she be eighty-three years old?

But just like that, Adriana pushed her forward and Fiona assumed it was time to sing. She cleared her throat, took a deep breath, and began.

"Happy birthday to—"

The woman, however, stretched out her arm and placed a cold hand over Fiona's mouth.

"There's no need for that," she whispered.

Fiona jerked away from the woman's icy touch and bumped into Mr. Stoker in the process. The man had moved very close behind her. Fiona couldn't slip past him.

"W-what's going on?" she demanded.

The woman cackled cruelly, revealing two very large fangs in her mouth. Her eyes blazed like red rubies.

Fiona shrieked, realizing the truth too late.

Adriana's grandmother was a vampire!

"What a delicious gift!" Granny howled. "After I eat, I will be thirteen years younger!"

Then she lunged forward with shocking speed and snatched Fiona in her cold, undead hands.

The End

Twelve:
Something Stinky This Way Comes

Jacqueline Hamm burrowed into the safety of her sleeping bag and yanked the covers up over her head.

More importantly, up over her nose.

"Whew!" she exclaimed. "Something stinks! Ally, was that you?!"

"Hey!" Allyson said, pretending to be outraged. "It wasn't me! She who smelt it dealt it!"

Suddenly a pillow launched into the air and smacked Jacqueline full in the face.

"Keep it down," Hannah, the third girl in the tent, snapped. "I'm trying to sleep." Then she sat up quickly and pinched her nose. "Eww, what's that smell?"

Jacqueline hurled the pillow back. "Ally is trying to fill our tent with poison gas," she said.

"Whatever!" Ally huffed. "A skunk must have walked by our tent. It wasn't me, I swear!"

"I think it smells like a whole herd of skunks walked by," Hannah muttered nasally, still holding her nose.

"Or maybe it was your boyfriend," Jacqueline teased. Once she started cracking jokes, she didn't know when to stop.

"Very funny—not!" Hannah said, but she wasn't really in the mood for trading insults. The awful smell was intensifying and her eyes were starting to water. The stench reminded her of dirty socks and unwashed feet.

"What did you two eat for dinner—stink steak?" Jacqueline taunted her friends. "It smells like—"

Two pillows whacked her this time, one each from Ally and Hannah.

"Enough!" the girls shouted in unison.

"Okay, okay!" Jacqueline apologized, shoving the pillows aside. "I was just trying to have fun. I hate that this is the last night of our trip."

Allyson and Hannah could relate to that. The three friends had been camping in the Everglades for five days. Tomorrow morning they and the other campers would go home. It was an eight-hour bus trip to Tallahassee, but totally worth it. The girls had had a great time.

Sharing a tent with friends wasn't the best part, either. The Everglades offered more than the girls had imagined. They had ridden fan-propelled airboats across the waterways and had seen pythons, alligators, and even an elusive Florida panther that inhabited the lush wetlands.

They would never forget everything they had seen.

Or what they were going to see that night.

"How are we going to sleep with that stink in our tent?" Ally wondered.

"I can try unzipping the door flap," Hannah offered. "Maybe some fresh air will help."

But as she reached for the zipper, a series of deep grunts disturbed the quiet of the night.

The girls froze. "W-what was that?" Allyson asked in a whisper.

"Maybe the skunk that sprayed our tent is back," Hannah said doubtfully.

"Nah, it's probably your boyfriend again," Jacqueline joked. "I bet he's here to take you on a stinky moonlit stroll."

"*Shhh!*" Allyson hissed. "Listen."

The girls held their breath and huddled close together without making a sound. The terrible stench was so strong now that it hurt to breathe.

Seconds ticked by. Another grunt came from the dark, closer this time.

"That sounded like—" Hannah started to say. But a massive shadow fell over the tent and she inhaled sharply, swallowing her words. The moonlit tent became as black as a tomb.

"*That's not a skunk*," she mouthed silently.

Her friends nodded just as silently and clutched their sleeping bags up to their chins. All three of them fearfully wondered the same thing.

What was outside their tent?

The shadowy figure sniffed loudly as if searching for something by scent.

Finally Jacqueline couldn't take the suspense anymore.

"Go away!" she shouted. "Scram! You smell like the boys' bathroom!"

The sniffing stopped and a haunting silence filled the air. But the girls weren't fooled. They knew they weren't alone.

"We know you're out there!" Jacqueline yelled.

A sharp, terrifying screech pierced the night in response. It was high-pitched and oddly ape-like. It also sounded angry. Then a stomp of heavy footfalls thundered away from their tent and slowly faded.

The shadowy figure—whatever it was—was gone.

"That was freaky," Jacqueline said slowly. "You two froze like scared bunnies."

"At least we didn't shriek like three-year-olds," Hannah objected. "'*Go away! Scram!*' I want my mommy!"

Jacqueline snorted. "Do you think being quiet helped? Next time you can try scaring off the monster by yourself."

"*Next time?*" Ally interjected. "Do you think it will come back?"

"Maybe," Jacqueline shrugged. "I don't know. I don't even know what it was."

"I do," Hannah whispered.

Jacqueline and Allyson stopped arguing and looked at her.

"Well?" Jacqueline prodded after a moment.

Hannah swallowed slowly, searching for courage. "It was a skunk ape."

Silence filled the tent after she spoke and tense seconds passed. No one moved until Jacqueline laughed.

"*You're* a skunk ape," she cackled.

"Am not," Hannah countered.

"You could have fooled me," Jacqueline sniffed, waving a hand in front of her nose.

"Stop it, both of you!" Allyson scolded them. "If it really

was a skunk ape, we have to do something. Quit goofing around."

The skunk ape was a legendary monster in Florida, similar to Bigfoot in northern states. Sightings of the unusually foul-smelling beast had been reported for decades.

"You don't believe her, do you?" Jacqueline asked. "A skunk ape! Was it riding on the back of the Loch Ness Monster too?"

"I'm serious," Hannah said. "Think about it. It gave off a horrible smell and made gorilla noises. What else could it be?"

"She's right," Allyson nodded. "It wasn't a skunk, Jackie."

Jacqueline blinked. No one but her two best friends ever called her Jackie. Not even her family. So when her friends used it, Jacqueline knew it was time to listen.

"Okay, fine," she said, becoming serious. "Do you think we should tell someone? Like a camp counselor?"

"No one will believe us," Hannah said, rummaging through her bags. "You didn't even believe us. We're going to need proof."

"What kind of proof?"

"This kind," Hannah announced, pulling a digital camera from her bag.

"You're going after it?" Jacqueline gasped. "In the dark? You're crazy!"

Ally, though, was grinning and pulling on her shoes. "Don't go without me."

Jacqueline made a strangled noise. "Don't you know what happens to girls that go looking for monsters? They don't come back! You'd know that if you watched more TV."

Hannah rolled her eyes. "Are you coming with us?" she asked.

"Not dressed like that," Jacqueline said. "You guys are wearing tennis shoes with pajamas. You look ridiculous."

"*Jackie,*" Hannah and Allyson said together.

"No way!" Jacqueline said, raising her hands. "I'm staying here."

"Will you at least cover for us in case anyone shows up?" Allyson asked.

"Sure, no problem," Jacqueline agreed. "I'll tell them you went to the bathroom. By the smell in here, everyone will believe it."

"Gross!" Hannah said as she slipped out of the tent. Allyson followed, shaking her head in disgust.

Jacqueline sunk down into her sleeping bag and stared at the tent flap. She couldn't believe her friends were gone. They'd left her all alone! Who would she tease now? Who would listen to her jokes? Who would hear her scream when the skunk ape returned?

She shivered and tried not to think about that. She preferred to think about jokes. In fact, if she ignored her scary thoughts, jokes started to make a kind of sense.

"Think about it," she told herself. Skunk apes weren't real. They were a legend. And knowing that left only one possibility.

Someone was playing a joke on her. A prank! Maybe it was her friends or a camp counselor. Either way, she would get the last laugh.

She smiled fiercely in the dim light and laced on her shoes. She decided tennies and pajamas weren't such horrible fashion after all. Still smiling, she crept outside.

The campground was eerily quiet. The full moon overhead bathed the area in a ghostly, silver glow. No lights or voices came from the surrounding tents. Everyone else seemed to be asleep until …

A sudden shriek caused her to drop into an alert crouch. The shrill sound had come from beyond the cluster of tents. Had it been Allyson? Hannah? Jacqueline had to find out.

Still crouching, she sneaked past the tents toward the edge of the wilds. A thick wall of hardwood trees rose before her like a border between safety and the unknown. She scurried faster, her pulse quickening.

"I bet Counselor Stine is behind this," she said under her

breath. Counselor Stine was the camp's storyteller. Every night before bed, he told a different ghost story in front of the fire. If anyone could pull off a skunk ape prank it was him.

Past the tents a dark dirt trail led into the trees. Jacqueline took it without slowing.

She had been on the trail numerous times during daylight. To her dismay, it looked completely different at night. The familiar sights were swallowed in shadow. Jacqueline felt more alone than ever.

"*Hannah!*"

Allyson's terrified scream tore through the night. Jacqueline started running toward the sound.

"Allyson! Hannah! I'm coming!" she shouted. In that moment, she forgot about Counselor Stine and his ghost stories. Her friends were in trouble!

She ran harder.

When the powerful stink of sweaty socks hit her, she skidded to a stop. The skunk ape was near.

Jacqueline bent over with her hands braced against her knees. Her chest heaved. Her breath came in gasps.

"Hannah ... Ally?" she whispered between breaths. "Can you hear me?"

She heard no response from her friends.

The skunk ape lumbered into view instead.

The shaggy beast appeared from the brush along the trail. It stood over seven feet tall on two legs. It had the face of an overgrown chimpanzee with long canine teeth in its snarling mouth.

Jacqueline had been told that skunk apes were brown. This specimen, however, had dingy white fur and a black stripe down its back. Strange, but it made sense to her. The ape was named after a skunk, after all.

She and the monster stared at each other. Jacqueline was too frightened to move, and the ape seemed to be sizing her up.

She imagined its thoughts. *Was she a threat? Was she alone? Would she taste good dipped in ketchup?*

Her eyes traveled up and down the hulking creature. Her mind focused on one thought, "RUN!" Until she saw the shoe.

Ally's left shoe. The skunk ape clutched it carelessly in a massive paw.

The ape's thick lips twisted momentarily in a kind of grin. Then with a flip of its hairy, muscled arm, it tossed the shoe into its mouth. *Chomp!* Just like a piece of popcorn.

Jacqueline screamed. That shoe was all that was left of her friends. The skunk ape had eaten them!

Still screaming, she fled. Not back down the trail and not toward camp. She ran blindly into the brush.

"Jackie, up here!"

Jacqueline slid to a stop, stumbling to her knees. As she went down, her eyes went up.

There! She spotted them. Her friends were alive! Hannah and Allyson clung to the branches of a cypress about fifteen feet above the ground.

For some reason, both of the girls were barefoot.

"We're safe!" Hannah shouted.

"Get up here!" Allyson cried.

Jacqueline pushed herself up from the damp ground. "Give me a hand!" she gasped. "Help!"

Before either girl in the tree could respond, the skunk ape came into view. When it saw the girls, the beast spread its arms, stuck out its chest, and roared.

Brr-RAWR!

The sight and sound were awful. But the smell was worse.

The stink of a thousand dirty shoes blasted Jacqueline in the face. She fell under the wicked wind and landed on her backside. The awful fumes left her gasping.

Before she could catch her breath, the skunk ape closed the distance between them. It reached for her with large wrinkled hands.

Jacqueline screamed again and twisted onto her belly. She kicked and clawed at the ground, trying to escape. She wouldn't let the monster get her without a fight!

Somehow she reached the tree her friends were in and started to drag herself upward. Hannah and Ally grabbed her shoulders and arms, pulling with all their strength.

"We got you!" Allyson said.

"So does the skunk ape!" Jacqueline yelled.

The beast's hand had closed around her right foot. With a sharp yank, it ripped off her shoe.

"Pull harder!" Jacqueline screamed at her friends. "It's trying to eat me!"

The monster grabbed her again, this time by the left foot. Jacqueline felt herself slipping. She was going to fall! The skunk ape was too strong.

In desperation she jerked her leg, and her remaining shoe came loose. The monster also let go.

Jacqueline was free!

With her friends' help, she scrambled higher into the tree. When she was out of the skunk ape's reach, the three panting girls stared down at the beast.

"What's it doing?" Jacqueline wondered.

The skunk ape raised Jacqueline's left shoe to its flat nose and inhaled noisily, a greedy sound. It sniffed the shoe's sole, laces, and worn interior. Then it popped the shoe into its mouth and started to chew. It swallowed quickly, let out a satisfied belch, and shambled off into the night.

"So that's why it smells so bad," Jacqueline said after a time. "It eats stinky shoes."

Nevertheless, the girls remained in the tree, hoping the skunk ape wouldn't return.

The End

Thirteen:
Exhausted Birthday

Cape Canaveral, FL
March 31, 3:19 pm

After entering the house, Robert Watts dropped his book bag by the front door and tromped heavily into the kitchen. He found his mother there, preparing tonight's special dinner.

"Happy birthday, honey," she greeted him. "Did you have a nice day at school?"

Robert shrugged. "It was alright, I guess," he said sluggishly. "I've just felt so tired all day. I think I'm getting sick or something."

"Don't be silly," his mother smiled. "You've never been sick a day in your life. You're too special."

He shook his head in disagreement. Too special to get

sick? Everyone got sick sometime. His mother, always his biggest fan, was the one being silly.

"Don't worry about it," Mrs. Watts continued. "I'm cooking something that will make you feel better. It's your favorite dinner."

"Lasagna?" Robert perked up.

"With extra cheese and sausage," she nodded. "Greasy—just the way you like it."

"Awesome!"

"See? Mom knows how to keep your motor running."

In fact, Mrs. Watts knew more than that. She knew how to spoil her son on his birthday. For breakfast she had served him pancakes swimming in syrup. At lunchtime, she had dropped off pizza for his whole class. And now she was cooking lasagna for dinner. Robert couldn't have planned a better menu for the day.

"Why don't you play some video games?" Mrs. Watts suggested. "I'm not quite finished here."

"Okay, Mom, thanks," Robert said. "You rock."

Still feeling worn out, he dragged himself into the living room and flopped onto the couch. The TV's remote control sat inches from his hand, but he didn't reach for it. Doing so seemed like too much work. He had only enough energy to rest.

Whew! Something was wrong, no matter what his mother said. Robert was too tired to play video games. If he wasn't sick, why else would he decline to play video games on his birthday?

The front door opened forty-five minutes later, and Robert blinked his eyes groggily. He had been dozing.

"Happy birthday, kiddo," his dad beamed, striding into the living room. "You're the big one-three. A teenager! How does it feel?"

"Sleepy," Robert answered honestly. "How was work?"

Mr. Watts smiled. "Exciting! Today I sunbathed on Mercury before going snow skiing on Neptune."

Robert wanted to laugh at his father's joke, but all that came out was a sort of snort. Mr. Watts worked for NASA— the National Aeronautics and Space Administration—at the Kennedy Space Center. He was always making goofy jokes about outer space and aliens.

"Cheer up!" Mr. Watts said. "This will get you moving. Look!"

From the pocket of his suit coat, Mr. Watts produced a small box wrapped in crisp blue paper. Nothing too fancy, just a neat package the size of a juice box.

Last year Robert's parents had given him a new Playstation video game system. The year before, an iPod. This year he was hoping for a cellphone. Considering the size of the box his father held, the chances were looking good.

Mr. Watts handed the gift to Robert.

"Thanks. Can I open it now?" Robert asked.

"Let's wait for your mother."

"Give me two minutes," she called from the kitchen.

Robert dropped the present in his lap and leaned wearily against the cushions on the couch. He could barely keep his eyes open!

In an effort to stay awake, he tried talking. He asked his father a question that had been on his mind all day.

"Dad, now that I'm thirteen…" he began slowly.

"Yes?"

"Do you think I could try out for football in the fall?"

Mr. Watts sighed. He and his son had had this conversation before. "You know the answer to that already. No contact sports, especially not football."

"But why?" Robert pressed. "All my friends play."

"We don't want you to hurt anyone," Mr. Watts explained. "You know that. We've been over it again and again."

Yes, Robert and his parents had discussed this before. And yes, he knew how they felt. He just didn't understand their answer or their logic. It sounded backward to him.

We don't want you to hurt anyone.

Weren't parents supposed to be afraid of their kids getting hurt? Not of their kids hurting someone else. Robert's parents had it mixed up.

"It's not fair," Robert protested. "Can I at least take gym class?"

"Absolutely not," Mr. Watts said firmly. He frowned briefly and shook his head. "Now, please, it's your birthday. I don't want this to turn into an argument. Here comes your mother."

"I hear the birthday boy wants to open his present," Mrs. Watts said cheerfully as she entered the room.

"Open it," Mr. Watts said, his former irritation gone. "You'll never guess what it is."

Robert tugged weakly at the wrapping paper. What could it be hiding? The cellphone he wanted? If so, he could give up on playing football for another year. Having his own phone would be worth it.

He removed the paper slowly like a snake shedding its skin. Inch by inch, one fold at a time. Was Robert moving in slow motion, or was the world around him? He certainly felt more like a snail than a snake.

He exhaled in relief when the last of the paper slithered off the present. Now he clutched a plain cardboard box mummy-wrapped in packaging tape. What was inside—a solid gold bar? His parents had wrapped the box as if it contained an extremely valuable object.

The prospect of struggling to remove the tape exhausted him. Birthdays weren't supposed to be this difficult. He exhaled heavily and closed his eyes.

Sitting next to him, his mother placed a hand on his shoulder. She glanced fearfully at her husband.

"Oh, Will," she said with concern. "Maybe we should have given it to him sooner."

"Don't worry, dear," Mr. Watts replied. "It'll work out. The boy has enough strength left."

Their words worried Robert. He was tired, not dying. But their concern seemed serious. Did they know something he didn't?

"You can do it," Mr. Watts encouraged him.

"Hurry, Robbie," his mother said. "Concentrate."

He did. He tried. His fingers moved lethargically but he kept prying and pulling. Finally the tape came loose and he tugged off the box's lid. Inside he discovered a small silver and black rectangle with three metal prongs on one end. The strange object looked like something for a computer. Written across its surface, Robert read:

NASA Experimental Battery Pack
Model #3-31-R0B3RT

Robert stared at the text, not comprehending. Why would he want or need a weird-looking battery? Were his parents going to give him a special laptop computer? Or some experimental cellphone?

"I don't … understand," he mumbled, his mouth moving slower than ever before. "Why do … I need … a … b-battery?"

"Now that you're a teenager, it's time you learned a secret," Mrs. Watts said, leaning in close to Robert. "You're not exactly human, Robbie, but you're still our boy."

"And this battery will power you back to normal," Mr. Watts added. "Better than normal, actually. You've been running on that old battery for thirteen years. It's time for an upgrade."

"You'll be Robert 2.0," his mother smiled.

Robert slumped against the cushions again. His parents' words repeated in his head.

Not exactly human.

Running on that old battery.

He processed their meaning and slowly understood. He finally realized why his parents forbade him to play contact sports. And why they fed him so much greasy, oily food. And why he could easily hurt the other players in sports.

Robert was a robot. A machine! He was stronger than everyone else in school. He needed oil and grease to lubricate his gears.

"You know the birthmark on your back?" Mrs. Watts asked. "The one you can't reach? That's your power button." As she spoke, she sneaked a hand behind her son.

"When you wake up, you'll be as good as new," his father said. "Then we'll eat your birthday dinner. And have some cake."

"Hold still, honey," Mrs. Watts whispered, one finger poised over her son's birthmark. "This won't hurt and it will take only a minute."

Click.

Robert's power died and everything went black.

The End

mysteryunderground.com

Read a scare ... if you dare.

Mystery Underground #1:
Michigan Monsters

1. Happy Hairy Birthday ... Walled Lake, MI

2. Night of the Tulips ... Holland, MI

3. Zombie King ... Midland, MI

4. Monster Bed ... St. Joseph, MI

5. Light's Out Lighthouse ... Alpena, MI

6. Screamer Stream ... Mio, MI

7. The Box ... Mancelona, MI

8. A Game of Bigfoot ... Marquette, MI

9. We ... Lake George, MI

10. The Catch ... East Tawas, MI

11. Knight Scares ... Detroit, MI

12. Field of Screams ... Ionia, MI

13. New Troll in Town ... Newberry, MI

Read a preview from
Mystery Underground #1:
Michigan Monsters

Happy Hairy Birthday

Walled Lake, MI
November 26, 6:47 pm

Cody Wolf peered doubtfully into the trees. He saw little in the darkness but heard plenty. Branches twitched like restless spirits. Leaves rustled, whispering in dry voices.

He knew instantly that the trees were nowhere he wanted to go. Not today, not on his thirteenth birthday. The woods always freaked him out in the dark, but a party waited for him on the other side.

If he could only get there.

"What are we waiting for?" his fourteen-year-old brother Brendan asked with a toothy grin. "You missed my thirteenth birthday party. Don't miss your own. Let's go, chicken."

Cody ignored his brother and squinted harder into the trees. Darkness stared back, and his mind shouted silent warnings for him to be careful. *Beware, Cody. Stay out. Don't even think about going in there.*

He knew he should listen, too, but the lure of his party was too much. Cutting through the woods was the fastest route home. It was the fastest way to cake and ice cream, presents, and cards stuffed with cash. As a bonus, it would also shut up his brother.

Finally Cody straightened his shoulders. He had made up his mind.

"I'm not chicken," he said. "Come on. Let's go through the woods." And with that he started to walk toward the trees.

Brendan clapped his hands together, impressed. "You're a big dog now, bro. No more little pup."

"Whatever," Cody grunted. "I just want to open presents before my next birthday. Now hurry up."

With Cody in the lead, the boys shuffled into the woods. Dry leaves crunched under their feet. Shadows melted together, blending into solid darkness.

Overhead, the full moon was a rude, pale eye, staring without blinking. Its eerie light peeked through the branches like a nosey neighbor who watched but never helped. Cody couldn't imagine a creepier setting.

The brothers walked without speaking for a time. They made it halfway through the woods. Then Brendan grabbed Cody's arm.

"Freeze!" Brendan hissed. "Did you hear that?"

Cody stopped and frowned. "Hear what?" he asked. He listened but heard nothing more than he had earlier—the wind, his own breathing, other unidentifiable but normal sounds of the woods.

Was his brother trying to play a trick on him?

Brendan held a finger to his lips for silence. In the moonlight, his normally brown eyes looked yellow.

Was that a trick too? Some kind of optical illusion in the dim light?

"Stay here," Brendan said. "I'm going to check it out."

Before Cody could stop him, Brendan turned and loped away back the way they'd come. He disappeared into darkness as if swallowed.

Long, cold minutes passed as Cody waited. He shivered and stuffed his hands into the pockets of his hoodie. He glanced up. Even the moon had abandoned him, hidden behind a cloud. Cody was as alone as he had ever been.

Alone in the dark of the woods.

Finally he couldn't take the wait or the loneliness.

"Brendan!" he called, his voice louder than he expected

and ending on a strange high pitch. What a surprise. Cody hadn't known he could howl like a wolf at night.

Cody Wolf, get it?

Cody didn't. Not yet.

When his brother didn't respond, Cody sucked in another breath to call again. He opened his mouth and—

"You don't need to yell," his brother said behind him.

Cody turned sharply, his mouth ready with sharper words. How dare Brendan vanish and then sneak up on him. It was Cody's birthday. His special day! Everything was supposed to go right. Everything was supposed to be fun.

What he saw killed the words on his lips.

Brendan wasn't Brendan. Not anymore.

A dog-like creature stood in front of Cody on two legs. Shaggy brown fur covered its body. Fangs as thick as fingers jutted from its canine face.

"Happy birthday, bro," it growled in a familiar voice.

To Be Continued in ...

Mystery Underground #1: Michigan Monsters

www.mysteryunderground.com

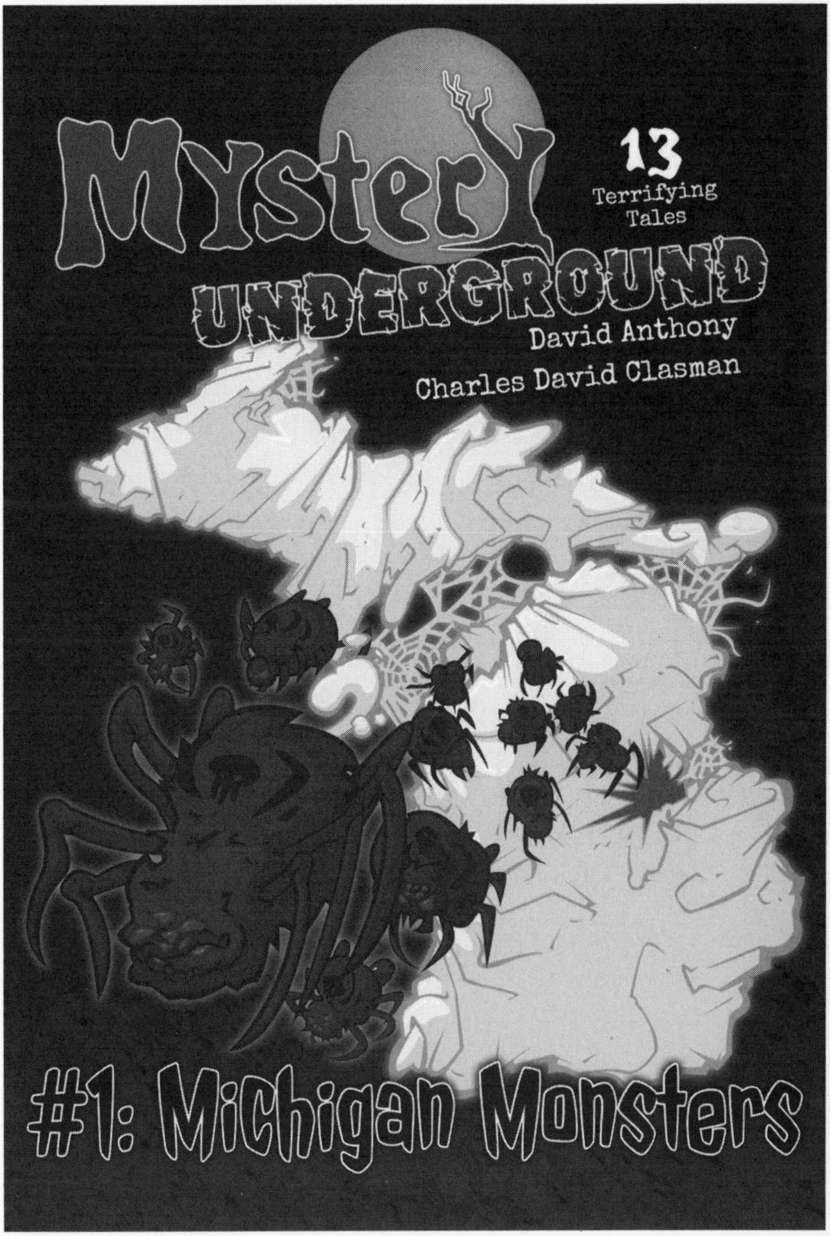
Mystery
13
Terrifying
Tales
UNDERGROUND
David Anthony
Charles David Clasman
#1: Michigan Monsters

Also by David Anthony & Charles David Clasman

Knightscares

Monsters. Magic. Mystery.

#1: Cauldron Cooker's Night
#2: Skull in the Birdcage
#3: Early Winter's Orb
#4: Voyage to Silvermight
#5: Trek Through Tangleroot
#6: Hunt for Hollowdeep
#7: The Ninespire Experiment
#8: Aware of the Wolf

www.knightscares.com

#1: Cauldron Cooker's Night

#2: Skull in the Birdcage

#3: Early Winter's Orb

#4: Voyage to Silvermight
The Dragonstone Horn Book One

#5: Trek Through Tangleroot
The Dragonstone Horn Book Two

#6: Hunt the Hullaerdeep
The Dragonstone Horn Book Three

#7: The Ninespire Experiment

#8: Aware of the Wolf

185

Also by David Anthony & Charles David Clasman

Superhero Kids
Fighting Crime Before Bedtime

#1: Alien Ice Cream
#2: Bowling Over Halloween
#3: Cherry Bomb Squad
#4: Digging For Dinos
#5: Easter Egg Haunt
#6: Fowl Mouthwash
#7: Guitar Rocket Star
#8: Holiday Holdup
#9: Ivy League All-Stars
#10: Joey Down Under
#11: Kung Fu Kitties
#12: Lost Puppy Love
#13: Monkey Monster Truck
#14: Nursery Rhyme Crime

www.realheroesread.com

Heroes A2Z #11:
Kung Fu Kitties

Moose Lee

Lucy Mew

Chuck Morris

Connect with the Authors

facebook.com/realheroesread

youtube.com/user/realheroesread

twitter.com/realheroesread

Email the Authors

Charlie:
charlie@realheroesread.com

David:
david@realheroesread.com

Lys Blakeslee, Cover Layout
lys@sigilpublishing.com

Lys graduated from Grand Valley State University in Michigan where she earned a degree in Illustration.

She has always loved to read, and devoted much of her childhood to devouring piles of books from the library.

She lives in Grand Rapids, Michigan with two bushy-tailed cats named Finny and Josie.

Pam Pekas Keith, Mystery Underground Logo

pampkeith@gmail.com

Pam is an experienced artist who has contributed to the advertising, marketing, and art divisions of various companies. Hundreds of her illustrations have been published in newspapers.

Whether generated on the computer or drawing board, her original artwork has enhanced stories both serious and whimsical. In addition to her illustrations, she has developed and designed thousands (yep, thousands) of advertising concepts as well as materials for major revenue-making marketing events.

Pam is a life long resident in Michigan and resides with her husband. She also has a grown son.

Michael Church, Cover Art
drakered@gmail.com
www.drakered.com

When not spending time training his Charizard or enjoying pancakes, Michael spends his free time drawing. A graduate from Grand Valley State University and Michigan native, Michael currently resides in Traverse City. As a way to alleviate stress, Michael will either watch cartoons or head out for some karaoke.

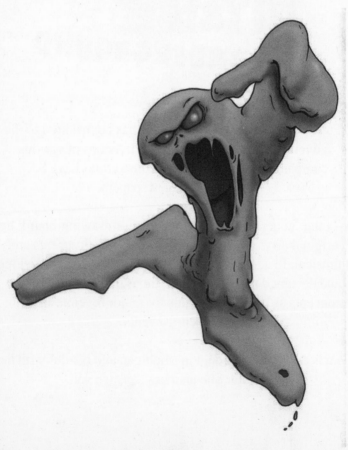